V. W

6/95

The Earl of Beresford stared in amazement at Veronica

"Are you saying that you have determined to make a match between your sister and me?"

"I cannot see that you will find a more fitting alliance," Veronica told him frankly.

"You do not think it possible that Rachel might find a gentleman on her own?"

'Oh, not at all probable," Veronica vetoed the idea.

"And what about yourself?" Lord Beresford asked.

"Me?"

"I daresay there might be the slightest chance that you would find a gentleman to meet with your approval...."

Veronica drew herself up to her full height. "Oh no, sir. You mistake my meaning. My plans are formed—and they do not include a husband."

DAUGHTERS FOUR

DIXIE LEE McKEONE

Harlequin Books

TORONTO • NEW YORK • LONDON
AMSTERDAM • PARIS • SYDNEY • HAMBURG
STOCKHOLM • ATHENS • TOKYO • MILAN

Published April 1988
ISBN 0-373-31019-6

Printed in U.S.A.

CHAPTER ONE

THE LARGE BAY MARE gathered speed and leapt, easily clearing the stone fence. The Honourable Miss Veronica Westfield maintained her seat as if she were part of the horse, urging her mount on, glorying in the morning. Her face was lit with the enjoyment of one who was savouring triumph over life and its fortunes.

At twenty-five, Veronica considered herself to be too advanced in age to require the company of a groom, especially since most of her riding was done on her own property. She was likewise too old to be riding *ventre à terre* and would certainly deserve and receive a condemnation from her sister Charlotte if that worthy young lady learned of it.

Her spirits were soaring, released from years of being burdened with the debts of a profligate father. Moreover, that very morning she had taken the first steps to bring the family fortunes back in tune. The purchase of a large, unproductive property and an investment of carefully hoarded funds had put her in partnership with a neighbour in the construction of a drainage canal. Well drained, the new and existing land of Red Oaks would increase its productivity.

Soon the near penury of the Westfields would be only a memory, though Veronica's daring still caused her to tremble.

Ahead, the sprawling stone structure that was Red Oaks Manor reflected the late-morning sun from the mullioned windows. The Elizabethan structure had mellowed over the centuries, and the oaks around it had grown until it no longer stood supreme in its height, but nestled in the countryside like a hen comfortable in her nest. Ivy crept up the walls, its dark tendrils contrasting sharply with the pale sunlit stone.

Veronica slowed her pace. No need to cause gossip among the servants, or Charlotte would certainly hear of her capers.

Several minutes later she entered the house by a side door and hurried up to the first floor. On the way, her glove was pricked by the peeling varnish on the stair rail, but she was too excited to get irritated over the pulled thread. She hurried toward the green gallery, pulling off her gloves, removing her cloak and hat as she strode along.

Her steps were those of a countrywoman in a hurry, lengthened by her tall, angular, almost gangly frame. Her hard ride had brought colour to her cheeks, and her dark hair framed an aristocratic face too long for beauty. Still the flush of the ride and the excitement glowing in her large brown eyes made her almost pretty.

As she removed the nearly new cape, the dark blue riding dress it covered showed itself to be of fine but sturdy fabric that had been overworn. Faint stains around the hem had come from mud that could never be completely brushed away, and the cuffs were nearly threadbare.

The green gallery was located along the southern side of the ancient pile, and its sunny aspect made it a favourite gathering place for the Westfield ladies. The appointments were from an earlier time, sturdy if not fashionable. The gleaming furniture and floor, the polished windows and brasswork of the fireplace hid from all but the sharpest eye the carefully mended curtains and cushions.

Veronica dropped her cape, bonnet and gloves on a *confidante* as she entered and strode down half the length of the chamber, calling out as she aproached her sisters.

"It's done! Tipton farm is ours, and Squire Larrimore has agreed to the terms. As we'll be supplying most of the right of way, the main outlay of money will be his..." Veronica had been so taken up by her success she had not at first noticed her sisters' agitation.

Twenty-four-year-old Charlotte, tall and angular, a pale replica of Veronica, had been facing the fire. She turned slightly, her thin arms folded across her chest. Together, Charlotte and Veronica inherited Red Oaks Manor from their godmother, and since the death of George Westfield, they had carried the burden of trying to restore some semblance of comfort for themselves, their mother and their two younger sisters, one of whom was still in school.

Charlotte nodded absently. "Then Hobart agreed and signed the papers. I know you're pleased." Her tone was dismissive, as if the news carried no particular import.

Veronica's steps faltered. Charlotte had been no less excited and fearful than had Veronica. Only the evening before, Charlotte had paced up and down the fireplace in Veronica's room, asking questions about the purchase. Not even Charlotte's prim attitude had hidden her glow of anticipation. Obviously something of a most uncommon nature had occurred since breakfast.

Veronica's gaze flitted between Charlotte and Rachel, who was drawn back in a wing chair like a child receiving unjust punishment. She looked far younger than her nineteen years. She favoured their mother's family, and though she was of a goodly height, she bore it with grace. Her face had the regularity of true beauty, her hair was a rich glowing chestnut, and her eyes were a deep blue-green.

Not even strong emotion could mar Rachel's looks, and Veronica could see that she was undergoing some extreme agitation. Her head was lowered; she was absently pleating the folds of her gown.

To a stranger it would have appeared that the younger of the three Misses Westfields now in residence was being strongly censured, but knowing her family, Veronica was not under any such foolish impression.

"What's amiss?" she demanded.

In answer, Charlotte stepped forward and thrust into her hand a much written and cross-written letter.

"Cousin Henry is dead," she announced and refolded her arms, her hands slapping at the sleeves like the snap of a suddenly closed book.

Veronica's eyes widened in surprise at Charlotte's attitude. Cousin Henry Arnesforthe, fifth Baron of Grimswell, had been their benefactor since their father's death. He valued his solitude, and had not physically entered their lives, but he had provided the four Westfield daughters with an excellent education and was responsible for the well-bred horses in their stable.

The Westfields were sensible of their obligation to him, indeed Lady Ellerbrook had risked censure and had forsaken her daughters at Red Oaks to stay at Grimswell Hall for the past month when Cousin Henry's illness turned desperate. His death was certainly deserving of a kinder emotion from Charlotte than irritation.

"We will send our regrets to Lady Grosley," Charlotte said, the fleeting pleasure in her face seeming to suggest she, at least, found in the necessity of mourning an opportunity to forgo an unwelcome invitation.

Rachel raised her head, gazing at Charlotte thoughtfully, her eyes showing her awareness of the feelings of others.

"It must inconvenience Lady Grosley most dreadfully to lose three females at table on such short notice."

"We will immediately don black gloves," Veronica said, expecting an instant agreement from Charlotte, who was always extremely diligent in her adherence to protocol. When she saw Charlotte's hesitation she frowned.

"No black gloves? What can you be thinking of?"

Charlotte pointed to the letter. "You have not heard all Mama has to say."

"Must I read it?" Veronica hoped to beg off, fully expecting the missive to contain a minute account of the old gentleman's sufferings. She was not unfeeling, but reading about them after his death served no purpose at all.

"You need not!" Charlotte snapped. "I have re-read it until I have it memorized. You are aware, of course, that most of Uncle Henry's properties were entailed?"

"Of course, but is it seemly to discuss it now?" Veronica replied, with more reserve than was usual for her. She was astounded that Charlotte would even mention the financial details so soon after his death. Veronica had never considered herself as having the least sensibility, but she found the subject a bit too forward in time.

"Unfortunately," Charlotte went on, ignoring Veronica's desire to change the subject, "his town house and his private fortune were not. It seems we are to be the beneficiaries, or I'm sure the rest of the world would see it as such."

"We are?" Veronica stared at her sister in renewed dismay. Knowing something surprising was in the offing, Veronica sought a chair and lowered herself into it.

"Indeed," Charlotte said. "It seems that Mama will receive a very sizable amount, and he has set up trusts for each of us."

"Trusts?" Veronica asked as she saw Charlotte's lips tighten again.

"Twenty thousand pounds apiece." The words came out of Charlotte's mouth sharp-edged. "In trust until we reach the age of thirty, or until we marry."

"Twenty thousand pounds," Veronica breathed. After years of watching pennies, she could hardly credit the amount. Then the meaning of the trust struck her. She stared at her sisters, her eyes wide.

"Cousin Henry provided us with dowries!" She envisioned herself making her début on the London scene at the age of five and twenty. The picture was so ludicrous she could not hold back gales of laughter.

As Charlotte stared at her thunderstruck, Veronica visualized the two of them together and laughed all the harder. Their age, their lack of beauty and their gangly height would put them at a ridiculous disadvantage in a society gathered to launch young ladies who were just out of the schoolroom. Not even twenty thousand pounds would outweigh their obvious disadvantages.

"She is overcome," Rachel said and hurried to Veronica's side, pulling a vinaigrette from her reticule. Rachel tried to administer the restorative, but Veronica pushed it away, shaking her head as she fought to regain control of her emotions.

"The dear old gentleman," Veronica said as she fumbled in her own reticule for her handkerchief and wiped away her tears of laughter. "He could not have thought what cakes we would make of ourselves."

"He could not, for I had never heard he was lacking in sense," Charlotte said. "Though I am beginning to wonder about yours."

Veronica wanted to laugh again, but she knew she had severely exacerbated Charlotte's already agitated nerves, and she was never one to tease her sisters.

In addition, Veronica suddenly felt an overwhelming sense of loss. She tried to take herself to task for it, but the sudden depression would not lift from her spirits. That morning she had been so full of triumph. After years of living in penury, she had finally been able to take the first steps to putting the family on its feet, and suddenly her years of struggle and planning were overshadowed by the stroke of a pen on a will.

Refusing to wallow in self-pity, she tried to shake away the sense of loss and turn the news to good account. She forced herself to think of how the bequests would benefit their plans.

When Cousin Henry enabled the Westfield daughters to attend Miss Filibrew's Seminary for Young Ladies, he had set them upon a course that was in direct opposition to the necessity of dowries. When Veronica and Charlotte met Miss Filibrew, they found their future in their desire to emulate that strong-minded gentlewoman's success. Like them, she had not had a suitable dowry to make a good marriage and instead had elected to make her own way by founding a school.

Veronica and Charlotte were well aware that their financial circumstances would preclude fashionable marriages. They were not suited to endless sewing and charitable work. Nothing less than active lives would do for them, and they needed to look to the future with hope. Since they were in possession of a large manor house that would serve admirably as a seminary, they decided they would some day open their own school. It was years since they had given any thought to a different prospect for their lives.

Veronica looked up at Charlotte, whose lips had thinned nearly to invisibility.

"Forgive me. I understand how you must feel."

Charlotte nodded. "It is hard to know such large amounts are ours and yet not accessible until we are thirty."

Once the shock had passed, Veronica grew increasingly pleased.

"But the success of the school is assured." She rose, clasped her hands behind her back and strode to the tall windows. Head back, she gazed up at the grey clouds rolling across the sky. "I have been thinking; because it is the fashion to learn Italian, we will need at least two more teachers. It will be comforting to know we have a financial buffer...."

Veronica paused, thinking she must make another visit to John Hobart, her solicitor. Her understanding of crops and property was adequate, but she knew little about legal matters. He might know if it were possible to borrow against the trust. That would allow them to begin the school two years earlier than they had planned.

"But Mama says there will be no school!" Rachel spoke up in accents of extreme distress. "We are to go to London."

Veronica, her mouth agape, turned to gaze first at Rachel and then at Charlotte, who nodded a thin-lipped confirmation.

"Mama stays at Grimswell Hall only as long as it takes to attend the funeral. And her directions are that we should be prepared to leave for London on the fifth day of the month."

"And there's so much to do," Rachel said. "I cannot see how we might possibly have three carriages prepared to leave in two days' time."

"In two days? This month?" Veronica voiced her surprise.

"There has been some delay with the mail," Charlotte explained, pointing at the letter. "It was posted Wednesday last. Mama expects to arrive home today!"

Veronica stared across the room. "I feel Mama is in for a disappointment," she said. "I have no desire to leave Red Oaks now." After years of planning, Veronica was looking forward to watching the progress of her first major effort to bring Red Oaks back to prosperity.

"Nor do I," Charlotte said, adding her wishes to those of her older sister. "It's nothing less than bad taste to drop everything and go husband hunting within two weeks of Cousin Henry's death."

Rachel added her voice to the others. "I don't want to go at all. Nothing could be more frightening than walking into a room filled with strangers. I should faint dead away and bring embarrassment upon all of you."

Veronica turned to survey Rachel. To hear the beauty make such a silly remark brought a tartness to her voice.

"More likely the swooning will be done by the hopeful mamas. They will see your entrance on the scene as the end of hope for their own daughters," Veronica announced briskly. "We must make our decision and stand firm. I feel for Mama and her hopes for us—"

"But they can only be dashed if we go into society and do not take," Charlotte broke in.

"Exactly." Veronica rocked back on her heels, unconsciously imitating her father. "At our age we would be considered ape leaders and be objects of ridicule."

"It will be a blow to Mama if we refuse," Rachel began softly, but her voice gained resolve as she spoke. "Still, I think it would be kinder for her to face a disappointment now and always believe we could have done her proud...."

When Rachel faltered, Veronica picked up the thought. "...rather than have us go into society and see us a laughingstock?"

"Which would mortify her, and that we cannot allow," Charlotte confirmed, straightening her lace cap with iron resolve.

All three sisters had been so intent on the conversation at hand that they had not heard the gentle opening of the door.

"We remain here," Charlotte said, her voice firm.

"I agree," Rachel said softly.

Veronica slapped her mother's folded letter against the palm of her right hand, adding emphasis to her words.

"It is decided then. We do not go to London."

Not having heard the door open, they were startled to hear a cry of utmost misery. They turned to stare wide-eyed at sixteen-year-old Miss Amabelle Westfield, the fourth and youngest sister of the family. She stood in the doorway, wearing a mud-stained cape and skewed bonnet; huge tears streamed down a lovely but tired face.

"You would stay just to make me miserable!" she wailed. "You want to remain in this horrible place and shrivel into old maids. You want me to die of loneliness!" With that, she raised her hands to her face and broke into uncontrolled sobbing.

The three elder sisters stared in silence, disbelieving. Until they turned and espied her in the doorway, they had full expectation that she was safely ensconced in Miss Filibrew's Seminary for Young Ladies more than seventy miles distant.

"Oh, my dear Amabelle!" Always most sensitive to the difficulties of any of the family, Rachel was the first to move forward and put her arms around Amabelle. She led her to a *confidante*, where her younger sister was allowed to make full use of the ministering vinaigrette and the offer of a lace-trimmed handkerchief. With gentle hands, Rachel undid the fastening of Amabelle's cloak and removed her bonnet.

The two other Misses Westfield crossed the room to the *confidante* and stood side by side in front of the younger ladies while Rachel attempted to soothe Amabelle. To have her appear so suddenly and without warning was as astounding as their mother's news. Veronica connected the two events.

"Mama brought you from school?" she asked Amabelle and glanced at the door, momentarily expecting Lady Ellerbrook to make her entrance. A quick glance at her youngest sister was sufficient to tell her she had misjudged the circumstances.

Charlotte also read the sudden wariness in Amabelle's eyes and was quicker with her tongue, her voice shrill with disapproval. "You did *not* return home with Mama? In heaven's name, how did you come?"

Amabelle's wariness turned to defensiveness. "I won't tell you! Why should I? You don't concern yourself over my happiness!" She dissolved into sobs again.

Veronica and Charlotte exchanged dubious glances. Rachel, who was embracing the sobbing child, looked up. Her gaze was studied and serious.

"If she didn't come with Mama, who brought her?"

"No one," Veronica said softly. "An escort would have entered with her." The eldest Miss Westfield had read the situation, and logic had provided the only reasonable answer. Even as she said the words, she looked for some alternative but found none.

"Am I to understand you've left school without permission, unescorted and by public coach, and plan to travel to town with us?" Charlotte demanded in accents of outrage quite equal to Amabelle's.

"How did you learn of it so soon?" Veronica stared down at the letter she still held. It had arrived only that morning.

"Our letter was late in delivery," Charlotte reminded Veronica. "She most certainly received her news from Mama with reasonable dispatch."

"I cannot think Mama gave her permission to leave school," Veronica said, not overly affected by Amabelle's tears.

"Nor I," Charlotte agreed. "At the moment I am far more interested in how she made this most unseemly journey. Her thoughtlessness does neither her reputation nor ours any good. It certainly won't help our plans for her to ruin our name...."

Getting her breath again, Amabelle raised a tear-stained face to Veronica and Charlotte. Her eyes glittered with anger.

"All you ever think of is your horrid girl's school. And who'd come to it anyway?"

What the two young ladies would have said to that is not to be known. For at that moment, the dowager Viscountess Ellerbrook entered the gallery, completing the family circle.

"Oh, my dear, so glad to be home— Why... what is amiss? Amabelle!" Lady Ellerbrook raised one tiny gloved hand to her mouth in dismay and hurried across the room to her sobbing youngest daughter. "My dear! How come you to be here—in such distress...?" She waved Rachel out of the way and took her seat as her arms circled her youngest.

Mother and child were quite a picture. Amabelle shared with her parent the fortune of guinea-gold curls and huge blue eyes, and was often said to be the image of Lady Ellerbrook when *she* was young.

Lady Ellerbrook had been the darling of society when she made her own come-out, and for years she had dreamed of launching her daughters into society. Nothing could persuade her that Veronica and Charlotte would not take or that Rachel's shyness would make society a misery for her. In her time, Amabelle could easily be the rage of London, but at the moment she was a very tired and very unhappy young lady.

"By the timing of her arrival," Veronica said, her voice carrying unusual censure, "I would say Amabelle has travelled home on the public stage."

"Mama, I think you must condemn her waywardness," Charlotte said. "I cannot doubt she travelled without escort. Miss Filibrew would never condone such exceptionable behaviour; Amabelle has doubtless run away from school."

"And so would you if you were put in such a horrid place, shut away from your family," Amabelle wailed, entirely forgetting for the moment that each of her sisters had taken her education at Miss Filibrew's.

"Stuff and nonsense!" Charlotte ejaculated. "And if you were so unfeeling as to have no thought for Miss Filibrew or for yourself, you might have spared a bit of concern for your family. It will be discussed all through the district that one of the Westfields has been brought to behave like a..." Words failed her.

At this, her lips parted to object to Charlotte's criticism, Lady Ellerbrook turned wondering eyes on her youngest daughter. Hers was not a mind to entertain

conjectures on acts that took place out of her immediate sight. Family loyalty kept the Misses Westfield
from actually saying their mother was henwitted, but
they had never considered her wise.

"Oh, my dearest! Should you have..." Unable to
bring herself to scold the sobbing child, she nevertheless cast doubtful looks at her two older daughters. As
usual when faced with their united disapproval, she
sought escape.

"Come, Amabelle, you are overtired. A little
rest..."

She rose hurriedly and coaxed the reluctant Amabelle, who preferred an audience for her histrionics, to
her feet. Rachel, still hovering by her tearful sister,
took the young lady's other arm.

"Oh, Mama," Amabelle cried as they crossed the
room. "Veronica and Charlotte say they will not go to
London!"

For years, particularly after her husband's death,
Lady Ellerbrook had deferred to her older daughters,
being slightly in awe of Veronica's capabilities and
Charlotte's disapproving gaze. But there comes a time
when one is cornered and must make a stand, and
Lady Ellerbrook had reached that point. She stopped
abruptly, removed her hand from Amabelle's arm,
and in ringing accents ordered Rachel to lead the child
to her chambers.

Then, resembling nothing so much as a bantam hen
with ruffled feathers, she turned and faced her two tall
daughters, who still stood near the *confidante*.

"*I* am head of this household," she announced, the
trembling intensity of her voice resembling Ama-

belle's. "It is my wish and Cousin Henry's that you go to London!" With that, and before either Veronica or Charlotte could return an answer, she turned and fled the room, closing the door softly behind her.

Again Veronica unconsciously copied the tall, rangy stance of her father as she clasped her hands behind her back and strode to the fire. Her brow was creased in thought.

"I trust you will not weaken in your resolve," Charlotte admonished. "It's not possible that Mama can hold out against us."

Veronica, who never in her five and twenty years remembered her mother taking such a stand, slowly shook her head. "This time I cannot think you are right. Mama is resolved."

"How is it so different from other times?" Charlotte asked. "She's often spoken of our entering society but it never came to anything."

"Then, we were without dowry and the wherewithal to cut a dash. And remember, Mr. Hobart controlled what finances we did have."

"It would not have signified if she had made a determined push."

"But she didn't know that," Veronica said. "Now the power of the purse strings has come directly into her hands, and with Amabelle to back her in her decision..."

Charlotte made a rude sound, so unusual for her that Veronica turned quickly away to cover her smile.

"I could shake that child!" Charlotte dropped into a chair by the fire, her movements quick and thoughtless, totally unlike her usual stiff bearing.

"Possibly if you and Rachel and I approached Mama forcefully enough, we could send Amabelle back to school...." She paused as Veronica shook her head.

"I doubt Miss Filibrew would take her," Veronica said. "If we could only convince Mama this trip to London would be harmful to Amabelle at her age."

Charlotte was still unconvinced. "She has the proof. It has already caused the child to run away from school, and to travel in such an inappropriate... I shudder to think of the talk."

"You're reckoning without Amabelle." Veronica sighed. "She will soon convince Mama she left school for an entirely different reason. I fear Rachel will be swayed if she's teased by Amabelle and Mama. Amabelle's tears are always a trap for Rachel," Veronica warned. "I fully expect we'll go. You and I cannot hold back to the combined forces if Rachel bends to Mama's way of thinking."

A strider only in times of extreme agitation, Charlotte rose and began to pace with her sister. "I for one plan to make strong objections."

"Oh, I also intend to make a push, but we will not sway Mama with Amabelle constantly in tears and Rachel's sensibilities tortured by misery."

Charlotte gazed at her sister in dismay. "If you are right, then what's to do?"

Veronica's expression turned thoughtful. She paced, staring at the floor, but when she faced her sister again a decision seemed to have been made.

"We could use our time to good advantage, making contacts for the school. I had not thought of it until now, but we need to enlarge our acquaintances in order to bring in our first students. Where better than in society?"

Charlotte opened her mouth to object, sought for a reason and then reluctantly nodded her head. "If we made an excellent impression on the ton, we could get a better class of students," she agreed slowly. "But Mama will be trying to make alliances for us, which will be bothersome, not that she will succeed."

"So where is the danger? At least not for me. Tall and gangly as I am, who would look twice in my direction? Not to mention I am older by several years than what is considered fashionable for marriage, and besides—"

"I disagree! You are all that is amiable and pleasant, and have a fine mind, though sometimes too wayward in the direction of levity. But I must grieve for Mama," she said slowly. "How hard it will seem to her if not one of her four daughters makes what she considers a proper marriage."

Veronica's eyes clouded with sympathy. "It will be a severe blow. But have you considered there may be an answer to Mama's dreams? I've often thought Rachel would make a most excellent wife and mother."

"You would sacrifice Rachel?" Charlotte was profoundly shocked.

"Never against her heart," Veronica hastened to assure her sister. "But consider, she is still of marriageable age; her birth, beauty and dowry could ensure a brilliant marriage. And, of course, with Amabelle ready to begin her season in a year..."

Charlotte looked up, a rare smile crossing her face. "Mayhap Mama would be perfectly satisfied."

Veronica nodded, then gazed at her sister searchingly. "Can it be, dear, that you truly have no desire for a husband and family?"

Wariness akin to anger flashed in Charlotte's pale eyes. "I'll have no part of your marriage schemes."

"No, think, Charlotte," Veronica urged. "We have always acknowledged Rachel and Amabelle as the beauties of the family, but only a blind man would miss your striking appearance and royal bearing. Any gentleman with sense would be proud to enter a room with you on his arm. Consider carefully. All our plans for opening the school grew from the desperation of seeing no other course open to us. Cousin Henry has given us a choice."

Though Veronica's sensibilities were not keen, she could see that Charlotte was deep in thought, giving the matter all the fair concentration of which she was capable. Believing her sister needed a measure of privacy, Veronica turned back to stare into the flames.

Only the crackling of the fire disturbed the peace of the room for a few moments, and then Charlotte sighed.

"I'm too deeply entrenched in our plans."

"It isn't a decision to be made this morning," Veronica cautioned.

"My heart is given over to the school," Charlotte said. "But you are right in your estimate of Rachel. Only how do we convince her that she would not be betraying us by making a good marriage?"

"We won't," Veronica said. "We must leave it to her heart to move her. We will find a gentleman for whom she can feel a genuine tendre. She would be happy as a wife and mother."

Feeling they had worn out the subject for the moment, Veronica left Charlotte deep in thought and joined her bailiff in the estate office. Years before, Charlotte had taken over the management of the household, and shortly after Veronica's exit she thought of some instructions for the housekeeper and set about her domestic duties. An hour before tea she was making an inventory of the stillroom when she was joined by Rachel.

That young lady's stealth in entering and her shamefaced trepidation told her sister all she needed to know.

"You have agreed to go to London," she accused.

Dumbly, Rachel nodded, not wanting to meet Charlotte's eyes. "Mama has hoped so long," she said. "It would be cruel to refuse her most heartfelt desire. It's not as if we have to marry after all. And Mr. Pettigrew could certainly be trusted with the properties until our return."

Charlotte nodded, knowing that not even Veronica would hesitate to leave Red Oaks in the hands of their bailiff. The management of the properties was not the problem. "Do you feel you can attend the routs and balls and be comfortable?" Charlotte asked.

Rachel twisted her handkerchief. She dropped her eyes as if hiding her misery from her older sister. "I am persuaded I will be able to endure it if I keep one purpose in mind," she said.

"Which purpose?" Charlotte asked.

"Dear Charlotte, have you thought about Veronica?" she said at last, raising her blue-green eyes to meet her sister's. "Had Veronica not devoted herself to the welfare of our family at father's death, I shudder to think where we would be now."

The inventory was forgotten as Charlotte gazed at her sister blankly, not taking her meaning.

"What have Veronica's efforts on our behalf to say to it?"

"It is because of her that we have lived in some comfort and that we have been able to make our plans for a full life—which you and I could continue," Rachel said and more positivity crept into her voice. "But Veronica has devoted her life to us. She deserves something better."

"What are you saying?"

"That we should make a push to arrange a suitable marriage for her."

Charlotte found herself shocked once again. She was poised, her head ready to shake in denial of Rachel's proposed scheme. She was certain Veronica's desire was to open the school. Then she was forcibly struck with the memory of her most recent conversation with Veronica.

Her older sister had asked Charlotte if she truly wanted the school . . . or had it been a lack of choice? Had Veronica in truth been voicing her own doubts?

Once Rachel had spoken, Charlotte chided herself for her lack of insight. Her eldest sister could very well be fatigued with managing the family, of assuming the responsibilities of their fortunes, of managing their properties and riding out in all weather. Who had worked harder and who was more deserving of happiness?

She nodded decisively. "Seeing Veronica content in her own home would be my dearest wish," she said. "And if we must go to London, her happiness will be our prime concern."

CHAPTER TWO

ONCE THE WESTFIELD FAMILY was committed to entering society, the management of the trip became Veronica's responsibility. As she would be away from Red Oaks for the season, Veronica planned to spend her remaining time scheduling several months' work around the estate. She was willing to leave the arrangements for the journey to her mother. Then at dinner she discovered from the half sentences of conversation that the good lady planned to have their clothing packed and the horses put to the carriages, and to begin the journey therewith. Lady Ellerbrook had given no consideration to accommodations on the road or to what they would find once they reached the city. Veronica knew she must take a hand.

"... else we may find ourselves sleeping in a hayloft with the postboys," Veronica told Charlotte. "Nor can it be seemly for us to arrive in Brook Street before Cousin Henry's solicitor has been told we wish to take possession of the town house."

Lady Ellerbrook pursed her pretty mouth and eyed her tall, eldest daughter with suspicion, but even Amabelle, whose impatience knew no bounds, was in agreement with the practicalities. She admitted travelling through the night, as she had done when she left school, was excessively uncomfortable.

Still, in just over a month, the family was settled in a luxurious town house on Brook Street. Lady Ellerbrook had taken her daughters to every shop on Bond Street. Modistes and mantua makers went into a flurry as they showed silks, muslins, hats, scarves, and assorted slippers and reticules.

"I declare we shall be overwhelmed by tissue paper," Veronica told Rachel a week later as she and Charlotte sat in Rachel's room. Martin, Rachel's maid, was trying to create order out of the welter of garments.

"I quite agree," Rachel said, admiring a new poke bonnet as she directed her maid on the storing of several dresses, three hats and four new pairs of slippers that had been delivered just that afternoon.

"Mama will outrun her purse should this continue!" Charlotte's lips narrowed as she shook out a silver lace underskirt and handed it to Martin. Then, as was her wont, she took a seat upon a straight-backed chair. Her own posture was so straight that she caused the furnishing to appear slothful.

But with her natural head for business matters, Veronica had taken the time to ascertain the exact amounts of the inheritance and how it was to be administered. She dropped onto the tête-à-tête and laughed.

"I doubt there is much danger," she said. "Cousin Henry was much plumper in the pocket than we imagined."

"But Mama has no head for finances and never could hold household." Charlotte was not one to be moved from a subject until she was satisfied.

"She has enough blunt to cut a dash for the season, and once that is spent, she'll find herself on a quarterly allowance," Veronica explained, "neither of which is paltry, I assure you. She'd have to take to deep basset to outrun the carpenter, and that's not her nature." She extended a long narrow foot and surveyed her kid slipper with a slight frown. "But for my part, I will be glad when these incessant fittings are done with."

"If you've objected to the clothing carried into your dressing room, I have not heard it," Charlotte commented.

"Nor have I." Veronica smiled at her sister. "I find I'm exceedingly fond of fashionable clothing, and if I must do the social round, I intend to gain what I can from it for the school."

At this the other sisters nodded solemnly, but Veronica knew she was slightly twisting the truth. She did intend to use every opportunity to widen her contacts for the sake of the school, but she also had a lively interest in everything around her. She would sooner or later tire of the city and the shops, but at the moment she was enjoying the orgy of shopping after years of watching pennies. Now that she was in London, she was even looking forward to the social scene.

They were gathered in Rachel's room in readiness for going down to tea. Their choice of location was determined by the comfort of atmosphere occasioned by the familiarity of Martin. Having grown up among old family retainers, the Westfield young ladies were not accustomed to the servants of Grimswell House.

Veronica's and Charlotte's own apartments were now ruled by London dressers as befitted their station. Only Rachel retained her maid. She had shocked the family with her obstinacy, saying she would not set one foot into a room that was not presided over by her dear Martin.

The gilt clock on the mantel struck the hour, and the young ladies joined Lady Ellerbrook for tea. As was the family custom, Charlotte presided over the tea table and poured. She looked around and missed the youngest member of the family, who usually carried around the cups.

"Veronica, ring for a footman and send for Amabelle," Charlotte said. "She grows more careless by the day."

This last stricture was directed toward Lady Ellerbrook, who shifted in her chair, always slightly discomfitted by Charlotte's criticism. "Amabelle is taking tea next door," she explained. "The young Brentwood ladies sent her an invitation and I saw no reason..." Accepting a filled cup from Rachel, Lady Ellerbrook lost track of what she was saying.

Veronica, who had walked over to the table to accept her own cup, stirred her tea thoughtfully as she returned to her chair. "As fate would have it, she's the first to receive a social invitation," she said as she stretched out her feet toward the fender on the fireplace.

"Well, I am not at all comfortable with Amabelle's choice in friends," Charlotte announced. "She is still a schoolroom miss and there are far too many guardsmen ringing the Brentwoods' bell.''

Veronica shrugged away her sister's doubts. ''If I understand it aright, the Brentwood twins are Amabelle's age. No doubt, they take their tea separately from Miss Elsa Brentwood and her friends.''

They had not at that time formally met the young lady next door; the gossip of the servants had informed them Miss Elsa Brentwood was also making her come-out that season.

''But they don't,'' Rachel murmured. Then feeling she had spoken too freely, she began a careful inspection of her teacup.

''Rachel,'' Veronica said softly, but with the same authority that kept the Red Oaks retainers up to the mark, ''I think you had better tell us what you know.''

''Yes, do tell us,'' Charlotte urged. ''Martin has doubtless heard all about our neighbours.''

Rachel sighed her reluctance, but the straight gazes of her sisters, and her mother's nervous glances, convinced her to talk.

''Some of our people think it not fitting that the twins are allowed to mingle with the guests as though they were already out in society.'' Rachel was clearly unhappy to be carrying tales. ''I cannot say if the criticism is justified.''

''Mama, we must take care to see Amabelle spends her time with people of unexceptional character,'' Charlotte said.

Lady Ellerbrook looked up agitated. She had bullied her daughters into coming to London, but she could not long withstand the strength of character in her two older daughters. She had reverted to many uncertainties, yet it behooved her to attempt some defence of Amabelle.

"Since she is most disappointed that she cannot make her come-out, I see no harm in allowing her to form enjoyable friendships...."

"Quite right," Veronica spoke up, hoping to forestall a family quarrel. "Amabelle must have friends, but of the right sort. Lady Hamford's daughters seemed taken with her. Perhaps we could have them to tea."

"She thought them dull in the extreme," Charlotte said.

"Countess Lieven was speaking of several picnics and afternoon parties arranged for younger ladies...." Lady Ellerbrook paused and shook her head. They all knew Amabelle had scorned the events, saying they were for children. To accept such diversions would be to give up her determination to make her come-out that season.

Charlotte raised her long chin and took a deep breath. "This is what comes of not returning her to school. If not to Miss Filibrew's at least to another, similar establishment."

Rachel spoke up for Amabelle. "Oh, but to miss the trip to London would have broken her heart."

"At first that was all she desired, but once allowed that she immediately began to wheedle to make her come-out," Charlotte said with more censure than sisterly feeling. "Now to hear her, her heart is broken because she won't be going to the balls, so what have you?"

The argument was forestalled by the entrance of a footman, who announced the arrival of Lady Radley, Lady Ellerbrook's second cousin.

The baroness was a dark but fading beauty and possessed all the energy often found in tiny, attractive people. Once seated and offered a cup of tea, she proceeded to regale the Westfields with all the gossip of the ton and to take their futures in hand.

Charlotte sat stiff and disapproving, and Rachel took what refuge she could by moving her chair so she was hidden by a large candelabra. Veronica relaxed and listened to the involved plans of their visitor.

Lady Radley was a widow without children, and she looked upon the arrival of the Misses Westfield as an opportunity to bring out surrogate daughters.

"And by tomorrow's post you will be receiving invitations to Lady Cosby's rout," she said. "The season's not officially begun, but this unseemly weather has driven so many people back to London...."

Lady Radley's social influence brought the invitations pouring in, and a few nights later found the Westfields passing through the line to meet their hostess at the first large rout of the season. Lady Cosby, a notable hostess, had drawn the *haute ton* en masse.

The Misses Westfield soon found themselves in a large ballroom, made brilliant by hundreds of candles, and even the more colourful of the ladies' gowns were dimmed by huge bouquets and banks of early spring flowers.

Over a pale pink satin slip, Veronica wore a deep rose silk crape trimmed with silver lace. She was discovering in herself an unexpected appreciation of beautiful clothing, and the three modistes she visited had commented on her excellent taste. She forbore any suggestion of frills; she enjoyed the elegance of simplicity.

Her major concern was her bearing: being used to tramping about the farms and striding along with her bailiff, she considered her walk and stance more suited to riding habit and boots.

Charlotte had unfortunately chosen to wear a rather dull yellow crape over an olive-green satin slip, colours that made her skin appear sallow. Her pale brown hair and pale eyes seemed to blend with her clothing until no matter the cost of her attire, she appeared quite dowdy.

"I cannot think it anything but unseemly," Charlotte commented as they watched the waltz begin, though due to some close friends living near Red Oaks, the Misses Westfield were already familiar with the steps of the newest dance.

"It's beautiful," Rachel breathed, her deep blue eyes alight as she watched the graceful performance. Seeing her sisters' surprise, she coloured slightly and amended her remark. "Not that I would have the nerve to take the floor myself. When Myra taught it to us, it seemed unexceptionable, but I think it quite dashing when danced with a gentleman. It isn't for me."

"Nor me." Veronica chuckled, though her reasoning was quite different. She was honest enough to admit she would enjoy floating around the floor in the arms of a charming escort. But floating was the problem; she envisioned herself tripping over her feet to sprawl on the floor.

"You will soon think nothing of it," Lady Radley said, her fan fluttering with agitation at the provinciality of the Westfield ladies. "And when you are given permission to waltz by the hostesses of Almack's, it would be fatal to refuse."

Veronica had been only half listening. Purposeful by nature, she had not lost sight of her goal of finding a suitable match for Rachel. In her few days in London she had, with her quick and discerning eye, already marked the differences between the genuine quality of fashionable gentlemen and the Bond Street beaux.

The affectations of the skintight coats, the too-high and uncomfortable collars and the overly elaborate arrangement of cravats indicated to her immediately those gentlemen whose extremes in dress betrayed them as comers on the scene. While considering them, she espied across the room a gentleman in the company of a young woman of about her own age. She marked him as the epitome of what she sought in a husband for Rachel.

His height alone would have singled him out. Slim to the point of elegance, he nevertheless filled his clothing with a perfection that buckram wadding could not attain. His broad shoulders were encased in a garment of most elegant cut, and the preciseness of his neat, snowy-white neck cloth decried the lack of taste in the more flamboyantly dressed males.

While Veronica was listing his physical attributes with cold practicality, she was also drawn by his attitude to his companion. Quite clearly the gentleman and his lady were involved in a verbal thrust and parry. It was also apparent that a genuine affection existed between the two.

Since his companion was not tall for a female, she was forced to raise her head to make some remark, her dark eyes twinkling with humour, and the gentleman, tilting his head to return an answer, showed a strong profile much softened with pleasure.

Watching them, Veronica could not help but feel her single state with more poignancy than had ever been her wont. She resolutely shook away her feeling of loss and wondered who the couple could be. Having given her attention to some passing acquaintance, Lady Radley turned in time to catch the object of Veronica's attention.

"A rare sight that," she commented. "Agness Cosby will be so set up in her own esteem there'll be no bearing her."

At Veronica's enquiring look, she continued, "Few hostesses can claim Julian Abbotsley's presence at a seasonal activity," she said.

"Mayhap his wife is of a social inclination," Veronica offered. She turned her mind over the odd name, sure she had heard it before yet not able to place it.

"There is no countess of Beresford," Lady Radley corrected her young friend. "A gentleman less in the petticoat line you'll not find."

Charlotte turned a prim look on their chaperon. "I daresay he is finding his companion charming enough," she commented.

"He's with his sister, the viscountess of Ivors," the
baroness explained, "though how even she could draw
him out to a rout I cannot say." Her eyes sparkled with
mischief as she looked up at Veronica. "No one could
fault your taste, my dear, but I daresay you should set
your sights on a more obtainable *parti*."

Most young ladies would have cavilled at such blunt
speaking. Veronica, whose mind was entirely on set-
tling Rachel's future, was not one whit discomfitted by
the baroness's remark.

"Nevertheless, that is an introduction I would appreciate," she said with total composure. "But at the
moment, dear cousin, I believe the lady to your right
is trying to catch your attention."

Lady Radley was not the only guest at the ball who
wondered at seeing the earl of Beresford present. Six
people were privileged to know exactly what had
caused that gentleman to change his habits. Only two,
Lord Beresford and his sister, Lady Elizabeth, were in
full possession of the facts. Neither was disposed to
satisfy the curiosity of others.

Lady Elizabeth Ivors was a young widow just re-
entering society after a proper period of mourning. At
eighteen she had been given in marriage to a gentleman for whom she held no true affection. She had
dutifully presented Lord Ivors with two sons, thereby
ensuring the family line. A few years later, that elderly peer had rewarded her by falling from a horse
and breaking his neck. He had left her an exceedingly
wealthy widow, free to enjoy the pleasures of society
without the restrictions of a single lady.

By means best known to herself, Lady Elizabeth had recently purchased a blooded hunter coveted by her brother. A week before, bored with the inclement weather, she had arranged an impromptu and quite informal card party which her brother, visiting town on business, had attended.

Their banter had led to a wager. The stakes were important to both. Should Lord Beresford and his partner win the game, Lady Elizabeth would forfeit the hunter. But should *she* win, he would be her escort for the season.

Lady Elizabeth was desirous of seeing her brother in the contentment of a happy marriage. She hoped it would stem his interest in Corinthian activities. His tendency to travel on the Continent was no safer, with Bonaparte creating trouble. She chose to exercise in the card game what she considered the prerogatives of a loving and concerned sister.

She cheated.

The earl knew the truth, but she had placed him in an impossible position. To publicly accuse his sister of dishonesty was an action that must offend the sensibilities of any gentleman. To demand a release from the wager could only mark him as one who did not honour his obligations. He was faced with the necessity of paying his gambling debt with the full knowledge that it had been unfairly claimed.

In truth, though he strongly disliked the season and its social activities, he was not too much offended. His sister had reached the age of twenty-four, but her one short season in London before her marriage had not educated her to the snares of the rakes and fortune hunters, and her wealth would draw unwelcome attention.

He felt it incumbent upon him to watch over her until he was certain she had gained her social feet. Still, he had no intention of allowing her to escape unscathed. He had been in the process of informing her of that fact when Veronica first glimpsed him.

"Gammon!" Lady Elizabeth said speaking behind her opened fan. "And what, my dear brother, do you think you can do to me?"

By lowering his brows and narrowing his eyes, he assumed a satiric look. "Should I give away my plan? You would then know how to sidestep it," he had said with a tranquillity not indicated by a casual view of those rugged features.

"Well, do tell me when you have taken your revenge," Lady Elizabeth replied, unfazed by the threat. "I daresay I will hardly notice what you are about if you do not call my attention to it."

Not disposed to dance, they sought out the card room for a pleasant hour and then moved slowly from apartment to apartment, stopping to speak with sundry acquaintances. The third time Lady Elizabeth noticed that they were being carefully observed by a regular long meg of a young woman in deep rose silk, she commented to the earl.

"I'll wager you are in for one particular introduction."

"Oh?" His inquiry held little interest. He was giving his attention to a glass of iced champagne.

The fourth time she saw the tall young woman appear in a doorway, search the room and then turn away after locating the earl, the viscountess of Ivors described Veronica to Lord Beresford. And upon the fifth occasion when Veronica assured herself the gentleman was still a guest at the party, he became aware of her attention.

The Honourable Miss Veronica Westfield was so intent upon her plans to have the earl and Rachel introduced, that it never crossed her mind she might be attracting anyone's attention. In truth, the only reason Lady Elizabeth had noticed her was the striking gown. But Veronica was a single-minded individual, and once having set her sights upon a goal, she was not one to be easily turned from her purpose. Her major difficulty had been securing the company of Lady Radley and her sister Rachel when the earl of Beresford and Lady Elizabeth were free for an introduction. Rachel had just joined them when Veronica saw the earl and his sister returning to the ballroom, and she gently pressed the baroness into leading the two sisters forward.

When they approached the handsome couple, Veronica was not put off by the wariness in Lord Beresford's eye. She could well believe that he was much accustomed to evading matchmaking mamas. But once introduced to Rachel, he would find the young lady a most uncommon beauty, charming, intelligent and ruled by gentle feelings. When the ton gossip informed him of the size of her dowry, he must recognize in Rachel a prize not lightly ignored.

While the name Julian Abbotsley had inspired no immediate recognition, his title had done so. Anxious that no awkwardness arise out of the situation,

Veronica had given Lady Radley a hint to use as opening gambit.

She knew one did not usually speak of business at a ton party, but the proximity of a piece of his property to Red Oaks would make an excellent opening for a conversation. The possibility that he might be interested in joining a drainage project with Squire Larrimore and her was unlikely, but made a better reason for an introduction than the obvious and true one.

Lady Radley was interested in seeing her distant relatives successful during the season, so after warning Veronica of the elusiveness of the prize she sought, the baroness made no objection. With the aplomb of an accomplished matchmaker, she advanced upon the couple with the two young ladies in tow.

The viscountess watched their approach, but the earl was otherwise occupied. He was trying to catch the eye of someone in a conversational group nearby.

Veronica noticed his gaze and cast a glance in that direction. She saw several elderly gentlemen standing together, watching the dancing couples through their quizzing glasses. She dismissed her momentary suspicion that she might be intruding at the wrong time. Certainly the earl would find Rachel more interesting than some business associate or distant relative.

The initial greeting and introduction completed, the tiny baroness tilted her head to smile at the earl. "I daresay you and Miss Westfield are known to each other by reputation, since she tells me there is a likelihood you may be joined in a business venture."

Though his manners could not be faulted, there was about the earl of Beresford just the slightest sign of boredom at finding himself accosted by a pair of marriageable chits in tow of a matchmaker. But this claim upon his interest was unexpected and succeeded admirably. His eyes sharpened as he looked at Veronica.

Not one to be caught off guard, he forestalled speaking until he had helped himself to a pinch of snuff.

"Miss Westfield, are you perchance my secret and silent partner in a little vessel now plying the dark seas from Calais?"

It would not have been surprising if a young lady from the inland counties had missed his meaning entirely, but Veronica had a quick wit. She had also perceived the slight movement at the right corner of his mouth that suggested he was suppressing a mischievous smile.

Ships in the darkness immediately brought to her mind the suggestion of smuggling, which had been a subject often written on in the London papers of late. He was out to discomfit her, but she determined he would not have his way. This was a far better game than the mention of a business venture, an explanation of which would bore everyone but her. In an excellent imitation of Charlotte's primness, she raised her chin and thinned her lips as she looked the earl straight in the eye.

"It is the trait of silent partners, my lord, that they do not make admissions. Still, perhaps it is just as well that we discuss Major Carmichael and his endeavours, which are most certainly not in our interest."

The earl seemed confused, and Veronica wondered if she could have been mistaken in the name she read in the paper. Surely Major Carmichael was the officer of the coastal patrol who had been recently commended for having captured a smuggling vessel? Then dawning understanding lit Lord Beresford's face: he had not expected to be taken up on his gambit. And while he had been thrown for a loss, his imbalance had been only momentary.

"Aahhh," he said slowly. "I take it you have given the matter considerable thought. Am I to hope you have an answer to get us out of our quandary?"

While Veronica was never adverse to running a harmless rig, she reminded herself—with some little regret—that her purpose was not to attract the gentleman's attention to herself. Therefore, she drew Rachel forward, saying, "I fear I have not the wit nor the intelligence to answer the problem myself. So it is my intention to get the advice of my dear Rachel."

Though she was a most learned young lady for her age, Rachel was not as quick thinking as her older sister. She was overwhelmed by being suddenly made the centre of attention. Realizing her younger sister's confusion, Veronica chided herself for putting Rachel forward so abruptly. She covered the mistake by saying, "It is my intention to put the difficulty to her when there is an opportunity for quiet and logical thought."

Correctly reading Veronica's attempts to ease Rachel's embarrassment, the earl nodded with all due solemnity. "I will be most interested in hearing her solution," he said.

At that moment they were interrupted by a portly gentleman whose ruddy complexion and rubicund nose declared him a man of large and dissipated appetite.

Veronica had been witness to the earl's attempts to lure the newcomer into his circle, so she was now surprised at his attitude. He seemed to find the stranger's arrival an unwelcome interruption. In addition, he was having difficulty changing the course of his thoughts.

Then he apparently remembered his original purpose. His expression changed to one of bland amiability, putting Veronica forcibly in mind of a young scamp at Red Oaks who was never so innocent in demeanour as when he was up to devilment. The earl's eyes slid to his sister, and Veronica knew she was right in her assessment. He was conjuring up some mischief with which to plague Lady Elizabeth. With an adroitness she could not but admire, he introduced the Honourable Mr. Oglethorpe to the small group and in doing so, manoeuvred that gentleman and Lady Elizabeth so they stood together.

The Honourable Mr. Oglethorpe was well-known as one of the regent's cronies and, like many of the gentlemen in that circle, was widely known as an aging rake. For all her tolerance, Veronica could not consider his frankly assessing gaze and smirk of appreciation as he considered Rachel and Lady Elizabeth to be anything but insulting. Nor could Lady Elizabeth, judging by the fulminating glance the young viscountess threw her brother.

But the earl seemed in no wise discomfitted and appeared to notice suddenly the tune being struck up by the musicians.

"I daresay that is the *rolande* beginning. Forgive me, Bess, but I am by no means prepared to take to the floor."

The earl had left the portly gentleman no alternative in good manners but to request the lady's hand for the dance.

Veronica watched with amusement as, accepting the gentleman's arm, Lady Elizabeth gave her brother a blazing glance. Veronica's sense of humour was tickled when she realized Lord Beresford had solicited Mr. Oglethorpe's presence for the sole purpose of irritating his sister.

Moreover, when he turned to Veronica again, he assumed a blatant air of innocence in the face of her knowing smile. Her estimation of him had risen considerably. Life with him would certainly be lively and interesting, and should Rachel have the good fortune to catch his heart, she would doubtless find herself living a fascinating existence.

Having noticed the skill with which the earl had manoeuvred the party, Veronica was mentally attempting to do the same when her sister Charlotte came on the scene, bringing with her a tall, quite somberly dressed gentleman. He viewed the world over a high-bridged nose with a look akin to Charlotte's habitual expression of disapproval. Veronica found herself introduced to Lord Folkestone. Once the formalities of the introduction were over, Lord Beresford removed his snuffbox from his pocket, flipped it open with an expert movement of his thumb and offered it to the other gentleman.

"Never thought you'd get pulled into one of these crushes, Tommy," he said laconically as he held out the snuffbox. "Try some of my sort."

"Thank you, no. I've never developed the habit." The baron's refusal was a condemnation of snuff in general and all those who chose to partake of it. He appeared to feel a reason for his presence was needed and nodded toward four people standing some distance away.

"M'sister, Katherine, is making her come-out. On such occasions it's best that all the family be present," he said.

The young lady was buttressed by two elderly ladies and a stout gentleman. All four wore expressions of disapproval identical to the baron's. Even the most hardy of suitors would be frightened away.

As Veronica turned her attention back to their party she felt uncomfortable. Baron Folkestone's stiff attitude was affecting the earl's sense of the ridiculous. The quirk at the side of his mouth evoked in Veronica a trembling desire to laugh. She sought some sympathetic remark to cover her feelings.

"I admire such family feelings, sir," she commented to the baron. "One's first entrance into society is a frightening experience. You must know young ladies are fearful that they will not draw the attention and approval of anyone of note." Veronica added the last as a ploy to flatter the earl.

"There can be nothing more damaging to one's self-esteem than to feel no gentleman wishes to lead one onto the floor," Veronica continued. Blatant though she might have been, she was in hope her remarks might goad Lord Beresford into requesting Rachel's hand for the forming *rolande*. But Lord Folkestone immediately turned to Veronica and requested her company in the dance.

So unexpected was this result that her unwilling gaze flew up to meet that of the earl. She read, in the asterisks of laughter around his eyes, at least a partial understanding of her scheme, and the amused knowledge that it had taken quite a different turn.

He made her confusion complete by requesting that Charlotte take the floor with him!

Veronica could not lay the blame for the upset upon her partner and determined to pass the time in his company as pleasantly as possible.

"I declare it is fascinating to see so many people gathered at one event." Veronica smiled up at the baron as they joined a set. With her height, she often found herself looking down on the males of her acquaintance. "I am aware that makes me sound provincial," she declared with charming candour, "but in the country, we often feel ourselves amid a gala press when there are not above ten couples present at a gathering."

"I rather enjoy the country life," Lord Folkestone returned. "Though London does have its advantages."

"Most decidedly," Veronica agreed, trying to keep her mind on the steps, for she was in lively dread lest her inborn clumsiness cause her to trip.

"I am not much impressed with the bookshops of fashion," the baron confessed, "but by judicious questioning of several friends, I have found some little-known shops that cater to the person with the deeper intellect—to one who desires more spiritually elevating literature than is usually found in the London drawing room."

While the baron prosed on about the discovery of an out-of-date book of sermons, Veronica automatically followed his lead. As the the turnings of the dance allowed, she espied Lord Beresford with Charlotte. She gave a small sigh as she noted from his expression that he was suffering a similar boredom. Veronica hoped Charlotte's primness did not give the earl a distaste for the Westfield family.

Lady Elizabeth was faring no better with her partner, for judging by his expression, Mr. Oglethorpe was setting himself up as her cisisbeo. His efforts to sweep the lady off her feet were entirely missing the mark.

When the dance brought Veronica in view of the side of the room where she had left Rachel, she glimpsed her sister—or more precisely Lady Radley and her sister's gauze overskirt. Rachel stood well back behind a bower of spring flowers. On the other side of the decorative display of blossoms a young pudding-faced gentleman also faded from sight as he edged back into the camouflage of the decor.

Veronica thought how nice it would be if all the shy and retiring people could find one another.

But futile wishings would not solve her problems, she decided. She must give more thought to getting Beresford and Rachel together. In charm and tone of mind alone he showed himself a person of most admirable traits, not to mention his title and wealth. He appeared to be the type of man most deserving of the charms and gentleness of Rachel, but they must both be brought to see that.

CHAPTER THREE

THE MISSES WESTFIELD had looked forward to riding in Hyde Park. Inclement weather had prevented their early-morning excursions for several days after the horses arrived in London, so on their first outing the animals were fresh and restive. All four sisters looked upon the animals they rode as pets and friends as well as mounts, and were well-accustomed to their personalities. When Veronica's mount, Lady Wren, took offence at an azalea bush and reared with flailing hooves, they took so little notice of it that the conversation then in progress was not disturbed by so much as a gasp.

Those out and about early enough to see the Misses Westfield ride, were treated to a cheery combination of colours in the ladies' riding habits. In pale blue heavy cotton with deeper blue ruffles at the front of her jacket cuffs and a small ruffle at the hem of her skirt, Amabelle was a vision as she led the way into the park.

Veronica favoured the colour wine. Her outfit was of corded silk with gold epaulets and a wide-brimmed, shallow-crowned hat turned up on one side to show her glossy dark curls to advantage.

Charlotte insisted fashion must take a second place to the plans for Red Oaks and had chosen a dun-coloured twilled cotton for her habit. But even she, pleased to be taking part in a comfortable and familiar activity, was disposed to drop some of her habitual primness. Using her riding crop, she tickled her mount, Sinbad, on a sensitive spot behind the ear.

Loving the game as much as Charlotte, the big black tossed his head, sidestepped and pranced. He showed his graceful paces until both Amabelle's and Rachel's mounts, not to be left out, matched their steps with his.

Before they had travelled far, the Westfields were hailed by three young ladies on ill-bred mounts, which appeared likely to throw out a splint in any more strenuous a ride than the slow pace through the park. Though she had not had occasion to meet the Misses Brentwood in person, Veronica doubted that two other young ladies in society would be dressed identically and assumed, quite correctly, that she was gazing upon Nora and Nolly Brentwood in the company of their sister, Elsa.

Veronica was bothered by a vague unease as Amabelle introduced her sisters to the Brentwoods. There was too much dash in the fashions of the sixteen-year-old twins. Their speaking glances when they invited Amabelle to become a member of their party passed the line of what was proper.

Charlotte was also displeased. She had given Sinbad the signal to settle down, and she sat as stiff and disapproving as if both she and the animal were bronzed. "I'm sure my sister appreciates your invitation," she said, her words clipped and concise, "however, I do feel on our first venture into the park, it would be better if we stayed together."

"Pooh!" Amabelle tossed her head. "How can you be so gothic? Veronica says nothing against it." Amabelle twisted in her saddle to look to her oldest sister for a ruling.

Veronica wished to say she was convinced Mama had expected them to stay together, but she saw at once the gleam of moisture in Amabelle's eyes. It prophesied an embarrassing scene, and Veronica quailed at the possibility of Amabelle's throwing a tantrum in full view of as many members of society as had chosen to ride that morning.

"I'm along to keep an eye on the madcaps," Elsa Brentwood explained as she reached up, curled a strand of hair around one finger and patted it in place. "She will come to no harm in our company."

While Charlotte sat disapproving, Veronica attempted to force her tone into a semblance of approval she could hardly feel. There was an indefinable ill-bred quality about Elsa Brentwood—that tilt of the chin—and her eyes were bolder than Veronica considered seemly. She was not much comforted by the young woman's assurances.

Still, Elsa Brentwood was making her come-out and she was received in polite company, so Veronica reserved judgment and gave Amabelle her permission. But the sparkle had been taken off their morning ride and they continued in a far more sombre mood. Nor did Veronica find her pleasure much heightened when they were joined by Lord Folkestone.

If Veronica had found the gentleman depressing the evening before, that impression of him was doubled when she viewed the animal he was at present riding. There was about the creature a decided lack of spirit, giving her the feeling the poor animal had been cowed with disapproval until it would not dare even whicker without permission.

Except in their mounts, she thought him a perfect match for Charlotte. He, too, wore a riding outfit of excellent cut and fabric, yet like Charlotte's it was brown. The best that could be said of it was that it was serviceable.

Veronica tried to fall back to ride abreast of Rachel, but just at that moment, Sinbad, usually most amenable to Charlotte's every wish, balked and fell behind, leaving Veronica and Lord Folkestone riding together.

"I had not thought to see you on the bridle path," Veronica said to the baron. "If I remember correctly, you were desirous of visiting some library this morning."

"Oh yes, but there will be adequate time later," the baron said, giving his attention to the reins as he held the horse in tight control. "Taking the air before embarking on literary pursuits is conducive to stimulating the mind."

Boredom caused Veronica to gaze up the path, and she saw Lord Beresford and Lady Elizabeth riding in their direction. As usual, they were engaged in some wrangle and were so intent on their conversation they had not seen the approaching party.

Ahead, the path forked off to the right to join an intersecting trail, and by Lady Elizabeth's gradual disappearance from her view, Veronica assumed the small copse of trees was an island of foliage formed by a triangle of converging ways. Veronica eased her own mount toward the right, and so brought the two parties together at the fork in the paths.

Lord Folkestone had been involved in a lengthy description of the library and was unaware the turning was leading them into a collision course. When he realized his proximity to the earl's mount, he drew up abruptly. Sinbad, who was immediately behind him, went into another fit of restive prancing, infecting Lady Elizabeth's horse.

"I say, I cannot apologize enough." The baron expressed himself with utmost chagrin as both parties set about calming their mounts.

Veronica spoke up. "The fault was entirely mine. I daresay I have committed some solecism by turning in this direction?" Veronica ended her explanation on a note of apology, which Baron Folkestone vociferously disclaimed, taking the total blame upon himself.

But with a slight twist to his lips, quickly hidden, the earl drew back his head as if to better survey the young lady leading the Westfield party. "I trust, Miss Westfield, that you are better at steering a vessel than a horse."

"Oh, much, sir," she retorted, glad he had taken the incident in good part. "Can it be the steadiness of the ground that throws me off my stride?"

Veronica now saw another opportunity to put the earl and Rachel in close company and she determined to make the most of it. Rachel was in extremely good looks that morning. Her teal-blue riding habit was most flattering to the auburn-haired beauty.

So beneath her skirt, where no one could see the movement of her foot, Veronica nudged Lady Wren, attempting to pursuade the horse to back, hoping the conversation would lead the earl to follow. But while Lady Wren was amenable to the wishes of her mistress, she understood the nudge as a command to move forward. Unable to correct the error without obvious resort to the reins, Veronica was forced to continue down the bridle path.

Since good manners demanded the earl ride beside her, the placement of the company put Beresford in the lead while Rachel was still bringing up the rear with Charlotte. As she was far from being a consummate actress, Veronica showed her disappointment in this arrangement, and Beresford looked about as if to ascertain what had occasioned her displeasure.

"Is it my company you dislike?" he inquired, raising his brows. "Or mayhap you are worried about our venture?"

The word *venture* brought to mind their conversation of the previous night, and Veronica felt renewed hope. That glint was in his eye again. He was indeed a man who liked the thrust and parry of witty conversation, and did not forget the subject of one. And to carry on the running game made furthering the acquaintance so much easier.

"Remiss of me," she said, "but I have not yet had the opportunity to discuss the problem with my chief adviser. I do think, my lord, that if you would do so, you would pose the problem with far more adroitness than would I. And our difficulty might be more speedily solved."

Despite Rachel's shyness, Veronica was sure that once involved in an ongoing banter, her sister's personality would come through. Veronica was pleased to think she had hit upon exactly the ploy to bring the two together.

"Ah, but somehow I doubt she will as fully understand the problems of the sea as well as you yourself...." The earl paused as he gazed at Veronica's changing expression with some speculation. "Is anything wrong, Miss Westfield?"

"Um—I beg your pardon...no, quite all right, I assure you," Veronica answered. From her view of the path ahead, she had a sudden feeling the situation was not all right, but indeed was all wrong.

The copse was thinning, and as the bridle path turned to the right, through the trees she recognized several flashes of colour. The red she had seen was the particular shade worn by the military, and the pale blue could only be Amabelle's new riding habit. She bit her lip and fervently wished she could turn the party in another direction.

But just at that moment, they approached a bend in the path and there ahead was an intersection crowded with mounted riders.

In the exact centre of the crossing of the paths, Miss Elsa Brentwood was, by the movement of her eyes and the trill of her laughter, engaged in a blatant flirtation with two uniformed members of the Life Guard. She was not sparing a glance for her two sisters or Amabelle. The youngest Miss Westfield was at the same time riding away from the rest, partnered by a uniformed gallant. The path she had chosen was bringing them directly toward the Westfield party.

In lively dread of what Charlotte might say to Amabelle and the possible resultant scene, Veronica raised her hand and waved as her sister approached. "Oh marvelous, you've found us! And just in time. If we are to complete our busy schedule today, we must be heading for home."

Amabelle did not appear to be overly pleased with the company of the young officer, and Veronica detected a fleeting expression of relief in her younger sister's eyes. Then Amabelle realized how her leaving the Brentwoods in the company of a young man could have been construed. She dissolved into scarlet embarrassment. Attempting to cover her sister's discomfort, Veronica turned to Beresford.

"I fear we have dallied too long and must depart from this pleasant exercise. Would you be good enough to point out the most direct route back to Brook Street?"

Lord Beresford gave her the direction, and it was with some relief that she led the Westfield party home. Seeing his studied nonchalance, she had no doubt he understood what had come to pass.

Charlotte made no mention of it but she had been aware of Amabelle's activities. With more tact than Veronica had credited to her, Charlotte refrained from bringing up the subject until the family had gathered for tea.

Amabelle had been shopping with Lady Ellerbrook during the afternoon and had purchased a papier-mâché reticule in the shape of a Grecian urn. She was showing it now to Rachel.

"... and I am convinced the Countess Lieven, for we met her as we were passing Hatcher's, was carrying one so similar it could have been identical." Amabelle reached up, wound a golden strand of hair around one slim finger and patted the curl in place. Veronica was treated to a sudden memory of Elsa Brentwood.

Charlotte, who was in the process of slicing a piece of cake for her mother, eyed the frivolous reticule with some distaste and chose that time to speak her mind.

"For my part, there are too many schoolgirls aping adults on Brook Street."

Lady Ellerbrook correctly read both Charlotte's tone and the mulish expression suddenly appearing on her youngest daughter's face. She drew her own mouth into a moue of confusion and sought to take what she considered the easiest path by placating both sides.

"I cannot think the purchase of a reticule..." Lady Ellerbrook's objection faded away as, glancing about, her eye fell upon her eldest. Veronica was gently shaking her head and dropping her eyes in resignation. Her mother's objection had given Charlotte her opportunity.

Before Veronica could step into the breach, Charlotte was in full cry. Her account of the excursion in

the park proved her sharp and critical eye had taken
in every detail. She condemned Elsa Brentwood's
public flirtation. Lady Ellerbrook seemed disposed to
give the neighbouring young ladies the benefit of the
doubt, but when she was told of Amabelle's exceptional behaviour in riding away from the main party
in the company of a young officer, she could not accept the news with complaisance.

"Oh, my dear! I cannot think it well done of
you...." Never one to complete a thought, she allowed her words to hang.

"Pray, don't be too hard on Amabelle," Veronica
said, giving Charlotte a sign to hold her criticism.
"While she does not say so, she was happy to see us
come on the scene."

Her face full of trouble, Amabelle gave Veronica a
grateful look.

Ever protective of Amabelle, Rachel smiled sweetly
at Charlotte. "I'm sure, now that Amabelle sees that
they are not quite the thing, she will forgo her acquaintance with the Brentwoods."

While Rachel had meant her statement to aid her
sister, Amabelle took instant exception to it.

"Rachel, I could not think you so lacking in feeling," she said attempting a dignity totally new to her.
"I only left them to return to the rest of you." Her
tone, so unlike herself, lent a note of falsity to her
statement.

"You may say what you like," Charlotte said as she
poured Lady Ellerbrook another cup of tea. "But the
earl of Beresford must have been shocked at your behaviour."

"He cannot signify," Amabelle answered sharply, while tugging nervously at an embroidered rose on her walking dress, and Lady Ellerbrook's eyes widened.

"Since I am sure his feelings are of the most sensible, Lord Folkestone certainly will not speak of what he saw, but I cannot guess what he must now think of the Westfields," Charlotte continued. "We do not know Lady Elizabeth well enough to suppose she will remain quiet about the espisode—"

At that, Veronica felt it incumbent to intercede on behalf of the earl's sister. "I cannot think she would have even noticed—"

"But if she did," Charlotte broke in again, fired up by Veronica's objections, "and if she decides to make of it an *on dit*, think what it could mean."

Like all hopeful mamas, Lady Ellerbrook feared any evil chance that might bring upon her daughters the disapproval of society. With that spectre looming large in her mind, the expression she turned upon her younger daughter was one of patent disapproval.

Amabelle was relying on her mama's dread of her tears to secure her vindication. Seeing her mother's tightened lips, her eyes filled and she jumped up from the chair, spilling the contents of her reticule and scattering cushions about the floor. Her anger was directed at Charlotte and Veronica.

"You didn't want me to come to town and you hate me for it!" she cried piteously. "You don't want me to have any enjoyment at all!" Tears streaming down her face, she ran from the room, leaving her three sisters and her mother staring after her.

Generous to anyone in misery, Rachel rose to follow her.

"I think it would be best if you remained here," Charlotte said.

Always loath to take part in a contretemps within the family, Veronica added her voice to Charlotte's and then turned her attention to her mother. Once having shown total disapproval of her youngest daughter, she was now fast dissolving into confusion and guilt. If such a scene must be endured, Veronica felt they should try to effect some solid benefit from it, and to do so, her mother had to be brought to some firm decisions.

"Mama dear," she said gently, "I do feel for Amabelle. We are much engaged in those activities in which she longs to take part, but the Brentwoods are not the thing. We must give some thought to Amabelle's protection."

"Indeed, Mama, Amabelle's protection is the word," Charlotte said far more gently than before. "Amabelle is too young to foresee the possible dangers of the freedom allowed the Brentwoods."

"I have it!" Rachel spoke up, her blue-green eyes alight with an idea. "How would it be if Martin were to accompany Amabelle on her excursions with the Brentwoods?"

Charlotte and Lady Ellerbrook appeared to discard the idea, but after a moment's thought, Veronica nodded.

"Rachel may have the answer. I can see Amabelle throwing a tantrum when she hears of it, but if Mama will stand firm, Amabelle would soon grow used to the idea."

"I cannot think she will like it...." Lady Ellerbrook let her words trail off.

"I doubt she will like any restriction on her freedom, so what does it matter?" Charlotte gave Veronica her support.

"And she will soon find the arrangement to her benefit," Veronica went on, "because while Martin will not allow her to fall into mischief, she has never been one to carry tales."

While Martin might be the answer to their difficulty, confronting the volatile Amabelle with the stricture was more than Lady Ellerbrook could face. Just the thought of her youngest daughter's tears made the lady hastily put aside her cup, rise and head for the door.

"I will give it some consideration," she said, her first completed sentence in some time. She disappeared almost as hastily as had Amabelle and did not reappear until the arrival of their carriage to convey them to Almack's.

No young woman aspiring to a successful début could look for complete acceptance if she failed to pass through the hallowed doors of Almack's. Lady Ellerbrook had been, during her schooldays, a chum of Lady Cowper, and had maintained a sporadic correspondence with her friend throughout the years. She had no difficulty in attaining the coveted vouchers. Charlotte was unwilling to give the assembly the awe normally accorded by social aspirants.

"I cannot see why society should make such a fuss over a set of rooms run by a businessman simply because they are given approval by sundry foreign titles, the granddaughter of a merchant and the son of one who is nothing more than a civil servant."

Lady Ellerbrook was exceedingly shocked. "My dear! You will not say those things! I fear you will find yourself and us...." She allowed her objections to fade as she cast a fearful look toward the driver of the carriage.

But Veronica's eyes danced with appreciation. "You are behind the times, Charlotte. The son of the civil servant can no longer cast those aspiring devotees of fashion into megrims with a disdainful look." The powerful George Brummell had been forced to flee the country to avoid debtors' prison.

This conversation, considered most unseemly by Lady Ellerbrook, was now brought to a halt. The party had arrived in King Street and they entered the famous but unprepossessing rooms of the assembly.

They were hardly through the door when Veronica chanced to see the tall figure of Lord Beresford with Lady Elizabeth. They were in the company of a gentleman whose age, volubility and attention to the young widow indicated Beresford was again putting his sister into an amusingly uncomfortable situation.

Even had she not been anxious to forward the friendship between the earl and Rachel, Veronica would have desired to move closer, fascinated by the earl's schemes. She was thwarted by Lady Ellerbrook's desire to introduce her daughters to several potential hostesses. More than an hour passed before

Veronica was free to urge Rachel in the earl's direction.

She had espied the brother and sister standing together watching the dancing, and headed purposely in their direction. Glancing to the side, Lady Elizabeth became aware of her approach and gave her an encouraging smile. Veronica was within a few yards of them when the possibility of danger suddenly occurred to her. If Rachel realized the determination with which her older sister was pursuing her romance, the young lady might become shyer than ever.

"Oh my dear, here's Lord Beresford and Lady Elizabeth," Veronica said with feigned surprise. Her wonderment became genuine as turning her head to speak with her sister, she discovered she was quite alone.

A quick glance showed that Rachel had stepped aside to speak with Lady Cosby and her daughter. Veronica was thrown into confusion by Rachel's defection, but she could do nothing but continue. She sought for some reasonable explanation for so peremptorily accosting the waiting couple.

"I daresay you will be glad to know I'm watching where I'm going tonight." She spoke with a creditable breeziness she was far from feeling.

"That knowledge does allay my fears," Lord Beresford returned, "I live in fear of being run down while your attention is otherwise engaged."

"Just so." Veronica felt her tension relaxing. The earl and Lady Elizabeth were not at all high in the instep, and seemed to always be ready for a bit of levity.

"I try to watch myself," she said with a smile, "but I do tend to be most single-minded."

Without the presence of Rachel, she discovered herself uncommonly ill at ease, not at all helped by the silence of Lady Elizabeth, who followed the conversation with such humour in her eyes. Veronica was uncomfortably sure she had interrupted some game between the brother and the sister. She was seeking an escape when the most unwelcome of diversions appeared in the person of Charlotte on the arm of Lord Folkestone.

Veronica was interested in her project of opening a school, but she was not at all scholarly and it had always been her intention to manage the administration and limit her instruction to horseback riding and sketching. But knowing she would face Charlotte's censure, and wound her sister's feelings if she did not show a proper interest in her escort, she greeted the baron brightly.

"And was the library all you expected it to be?" she asked after the pleasantries of greetings had passed.

"I confess I found myself somewhat disappointed," the baron said, looking down his nose at the assembled company. "Though the sermons of the Reverend Hedgerton were quite as inspiring as one might expect, I did find a deplorable lack in the writings of Bishop Copthin. As you will remember, he was most astute in his observations during the reign of Charles II, particularly his—"

"Lord, give over, Tommy! You'll drive the ladies to distraction!" Lord Beresford demanded, interrupting Folkestone with more expediency than manners.

Veronica's gratitude was short-lived. The baron took umbrage at the breach of etiquette. He puffed himself up and looked down his high-bridged nose at Veronica. "Miss Westfield, if you would care to join me in the dance now forming," he said with awesome hauteur, "we can then continue our conversation without boring those whose minds are on lighter subjects."

Although she was in no mood for a discourse on the sermons of a bishop or on any other worthy's thought, Veronica had no recourse but to allow the gentleman to lead her onto the floor. Luckily, they were engaged in a country dance and the figures separated them long enough for her to form a plan, once she could secure Rachel's company again.

Indeed she was quite pleased to have thought of it. She would call upon Rachel's tender heart. They had seen the young widow three times, and always in the company of her brother. If Rachel were convinced the lady had no friends in town, she might overcome her shyness in an effort to give Lady Elizabeth female companionship. Veronica expected the lively and charming viscountess had a large female acquaintance, but Rachel need not know of it. The object was to get her into closer proximity to the earl, after all.

Once away from Baron Folkestone, she succeeded in drawing her sister aside and commented on the unhappiness she pretended to see in Lady Elizabeth. Rachel was sympathetic and hit upon the happy idea of making the season more enjoyable for the young widow.

"There she is now," Veronica said when she had at last located the earl and his sister leaving the card room. "We could invite her to ride with us in the morning."

"Oh I quite agree," Rachel said, and together they started in the direction of the bother and sister.

They were just approaching the earl and Lady Elizabeth when a young lady whom they had met earlier in the evening hailed Rachel to introduce her to her mother. So again Veronica found herself eye to eye with Lady Elizabeth and the earl of Beresford, while Rachel had been drawn away.

This constant thwarting of her purpose was beginning to grate on Veronica's nerves. Had she been at home at Red Oaks, some unlucky fence post would have borne the marks of her riding crop. Unfortunately, the assembly rooms in Almack's were not a suitable location for venting her frustrations, and the lack of opportunity to express her true feelings brought a hot blush to her cheeks.

Nor could she understand why Lady Elizabeth had suddenly dimpled up in almost unseemly humour and stammered to her brother that she had just seen a lady with whom she must have some conversation. The earl was nonplussed at this flagrant desertion, but he recovered quickly and suggested to Veronica that perhaps she would care for a glass of lemonade.

Since any occupation was preferable to standing awkwardly, abandoned by her sister, she acquiesced. She took the earl's proffered arm and walked with him into the refreshment room.

Like herself, he seemed preoccupied and lacking his usual poise. Knowing his affection for the Lady Elizabeth, Veronica assumed he was interested in seeking her presence, so she suggested he might wish to take his leave. But his disclaimer seemed to hold more than mere politeness.

"I daresay she has gone to seek out a friend of hers who must be quite embarrassed to return to society," he said, speaking with what seemed to be a hesitancy born of discomfort.

"Not that she herself could be faulted," he added, and it seemed to Veronica he was finding himself in some confusion. Thinking he had, in an unguarded moment, overstepped his own sense of discretion, she attempted to help him out of his quandary.

"One can innocently commit a foolish act and have no idea it will become a subject of gossip," she said. "No doubt people forget quickly, and they do forgive."

"Most assuredly," he returned. "Any person of feeling had to pity the lady," he said, doggedly continuing though he seemed to find the subject distasteful. "She sponsored her niece, a young chit completely lacking in sensibility. The girl made a cake of herself. She followed a gentleman around until he was in lively terror even of seeing her enter a room. All London was laughing behind their hands."

His story finished, the earl gazed down at Veronica with a most intense look, one she could not quite fathom. Having accepted his story at face value, Veronica nodded thoughtfully.

"I understand the gentleman's discomfort," she said. "It must also have been exquisitely uncomfortable for the lady who was sponsoring the child." She suddenly realized he had hidden a purpose beneath his tale. He had changed the circumstances for her benefit, but she understood. She sighed and smiled sadly.

"You have told me this story for a reason." Seeing his embarrassment, she tapped him lightly on the arm with her fan. "Sir, please forgive me. I feel as strongly as you the distress of your position." Veronica's heart went out to him as his eyes met hers; in them she saw the pain he felt his words had given her.

"You would notice, of course, but I doubt anyone else has seen in Rachel's defection anything but coincidence. I am assured it has not come to the attention of the gossips."

The earl appeared considerably startled. "Rachel— *Rachel's* defection?"

"Indeed, I am as vexed as you must be, for here I am spending my time trying—but no matter, I begin to think the cause is hopeless."

"The cause..." the earl repeated slowly, totally lost at the unexpected turn of the conversation. He stared down at Veronica, fascinated. But she, caught up in the difficulties of her plans going awry, did not notice his confusion.

"Rachel is always sensible of the feelings of others, and would not for worlds cause you pain or embarrassment. I fear I must give up all my plans. I cannot allow her to make you a laughingstock simply because she does not desire your interest."

Lord Beresford blinked, and appeared to be waking from some stupor. "She does not care for me—in spite of your attempts to effect…" He stared down at Veronica again. "To effect—I see." He gazed out across the room, as if across his imagination ran some extraordinary sight not visible to the rest of the company. "How unfortunate," he murmured, smiling slightly, though no humour lit his eyes as he gazed at her intently.

"Quite," Veronica said. "I must have a word with her, which could throw her into confusion, or I must give up the scheme entirely. Of course—" she paused thoughtfully "—there is another alternative." She raised her eyes to Lord Beresford and was encouraged by his fascination. "If you would just make some push to be amiable, I am convinced her shyness would soon wear off and we would go along most comfortably."

"Easy over the bricks, my girl," the earl said with a slight breathlessness. "Are you saying you have determined to make a match between your sister and me and I must also take a hand?"

"Well, I may be partial to Rachel, but I cannot see you will find a more fitting alliance," she told him frankly. "Our family is as old as any in the country; she is acceptably dowered, which I understand need not be a consideration with you, and in both appearance and spirit, you will not find a more beautiful creature."

Beresford nodded, but seemed not at all convinced. "May I remind you she does not care for me?"

Seeing he was put out, Veronica patted him bracingly on the arm. "Oh, do not let it distress you. I can assure you she does not hold you in distaste, either for your person, title or fortune. Her heart is somewhat engaged—not by any gentleman—but by family plans of long standing."

In order that he might not take Rachel's lack of interest personally, Veronica gave him an account of their history and explained in detail their hope to start a school at Red Oaks.

"...and this dowry matter is most inconvenient. We have worked so long and it is difficult to give up those ideas."

She explained how she and Charlotte had determined that Rachel would make an excellent wife. Moreover, Lady Ellerbrook would be quite satisfied if one of her daughters made a truly brilliant marriage.

By now thoroughly enthralled, the earl had been sufficiently drawn into the subject to pose some questions of his own.

"You do not think it possible that Rachel might find a husband on her own?"

"Oh, not at all probable." Veronica vetoed the idea.

"And what about yourself?" Lord Beresford asked.

"Me?" Veronica was surprised at the question.

"Well, I daresay," the earl spoke thoughtfully, "there might be the slightest chance that you would find a gentleman to meet with your approval—"

At this, Veronica drew herself up to her full height and shook her head with extreme resolution.

"You mistake my meaning, sir. There are many estimable gentlemen most deserving of consideration, but *my* plans are formed."

They had, at this time, left the refreshment room and were just passing the card room, when Veronica gave an exasperated sigh. Who should be approaching but Charlotte in the company of Lord Folkestone. Veronica determined that at the earliest opportunity she would have a word with Lady Ellerbrook. Charlotte must be introduced to other gentlemen: any substitute would be more pleasant company than the bore who was taking up her time.

Again, with no outlet for her frustration, Veronica felt the heat in her cheeks and Charlotte was quick to notice it.

"My dear, you are overheated," Charlotte said and turned imploring eyes upon the baron. "Sir, may I impose upon you to escort my sister to the refreshment room and procure for her a glass of lemonade?"

"It would be my pleasure." Lord Folkestone bowed over Veronica's hand. He left Charlotte with the earl of Beresford and led Veronica back into the dining room.

CHAPTER FOUR

JULIAN ABBOTSLEY HAD BEEN RAISED to regard his consequence and station. The fifth earl of Beresford had passed his sixtieth birthday when his first son was born, so it was correctly assumed that the sixth earl would ascend to both his titles and responsibilities at an early age.

A healthy and handsome child, he grew to be a man of pleasing though slightly rugged features, who carried himself with the unconscious ease of privilege. His innocence of pretensions was born of never needing to assert himself. When he travelled, which was often, his man went before him, so his wealth and social position were always known and he was catered to accordingly. Had he been questioned, he would have supposed someone must have puffed off his station, but in truth he had never given the matter a thought.

He was the earl of Beresford: his awareness that his position, holdings and wealth carried with them certain power was only vague, since he was not of a political turn of mind, and having no enemies, he had never sought to use it. He was tolerant but slightly contemptuous of toad-eating mushrooms and matchmaking mamas, and accepted the approval of others as naturally as he did his name and his title. Rejection was so foreign as to be unimaginable.

It was then not so very surprising that his sister found him in deep thought, his emotions a combination of wonder, outrage and humour. Not immediately recognizing her brother's mood, Lady Elizabeth coyly flipped her fan and eyed him flirtatiously.

"Julian, I cannot conceive of finding you alone. I thought your latest inamorata would be clinging to your arm."

"You are out there, Bess," the earl said with a semblance of nonchalance. "As usual, Rachel took herself off."

"I beg your pardon?" Lady Elizabeth looked at him with laughing curiosity.

Caught once again in the ridiculousness of his position, the earl suppressed a laugh.

"It is plain by your attitude, my dear, that you have not perfectly understood what's toward. It seems I am being pursued by a young lady who will not have me, for the benefit of a second young lady who will not have me, either."

Lady Elizabeth gazed at her brother, wondering if he was a candidate for Bedlam. The only other conceivable answer was that he was in his cups.

"Julian, how did you manage it? I know nothing stronger than orgeat is served in these rooms. Did you by chance smuggle in a flask of port?"

This question elicited a look of total disdain from the earl. "I am not foxed! Your grasp of the matter is less than perfect. I will endeavour to tell you how it came about—I don't promise clarification, but I'll try.''

''I wish you will. A more diverting situation at Almack's I have yet to encounter.''

And indeed the viscountess of Ivors stood wide-eyed and silent while her brother repeated Veronica's explanation.

''But I am assured,'' Beresford said tranquilly, ''that I am not to assume the young lady's distaste for me can in any way be taken personally.''

Lady Elizabeth's eyes had already opened to their full width. When she heard of Veronica's reassurances to Lord Beresford, she stood gaping with wonder.

''She could not have said as much to you.'' Her voice held total incredulity.

''How not?'' the earl asked as if his sister's doubts were unthinkable. ''Would you have her leave me totally set down with no hope that another lady would find me worth a second look?''

''Nothing she says can signify!'' Lady Elizabeth tossed her head, suddenly irritated. ''Certainly any female whose taste was nice...'' Her eyes narrowed and she tilted her head to look up at her brother. ''Is this some rig you're running?''

At that he raised his hands, disclaiming to be anything but the most serious, though his eye twinkled appreciatively. ''My dear, there are rigs within rigs. I bring you nothing but the truth as I was told it, but while Miss Veronica Westfield is engaged in arranging a match between her sister Rachel and myself, I notice that other, bluestocking sister of hers—''

"You're speaking of Miss Charlotte Westfield?" Lady Elizabeth broke in. Despite the convolutions of the problem at hand, she had determined to understand it and not lose a single, spellbinding turn of play.

The earl nodded with due solemnity. "As I was saying, I see that Miss Charlotte Westfield is most assiduous in her efforts to force Folkestone upon her elder sister."

For some time Lady Elizabeth had been holding her fan close to her face, lest her looks of astonishment and delight draw attention and cause conjecture. Now she clapped a hand to her mouth to keep back an unseemly crow of mirth.

"Is that why she drags that pompous buffoon about? It will never do, of course. While no one could accuse the eldest Miss Westfield of having anything but perfect manners—" Lady Elizabeth suddenly twinkled up at her brother "—save possibly in her pursuit of a gentleman for her sister..."

"That is not a matter of manners, but a single-mindedness of purpose," Beresford corrected his sister. "She explained that in great detail."

"Nevertheless, Folkestone will not do for Veronica," Lady Elizabeth finished.

"Your perspicacity is astounding," replied the earl.

"She thinks him a pompous bore," she further elaborated.

"For which we will fault her?" the earl asked with a half smile.

"Oh, most assuredly not! Unless..." Lady Elizabeth rolled her eyes to the ceiling with a thoughtful expression. "Unless we should choose to take offense at her lack of taste in considering a school more important than our august lineage."

"But has she done so?" asked the earl. "Do consider. While Miss Westfield made it plain that teaching young ladies is much preferable to me or any other gentleman of the ton, she did, in fact, consider me suitable for her younger sister."

Lady Elizabeth could not hold back a gurgle of laughter. "You've lost out there, also. Only a few moments ago I had occasion to see young Rachel in the refreshment room. Unless I mistake the matter, she and Mr. Tonley were exchanging shy glances around the large epergne."

The earl drew back, revolted. "Are you saying she prefers that—that—pudding-faced gudgeon to me?"

Eyes twinkling, Lady Elizabeth threw out a hand in resignation. "You have now been deposed in the affections of one young woman by a school and cut out with another chit by a shy young man who cannot find his way out from behind a potted plant. I fear your reputation is ruined."

"Gammon!" Beresford ejaculated. "I am not puffed up in my own conceit, but to be superseded in a female's attentions by that stuttering puppy—"

Lady Elizabeth laid a finger to her cheek with an expression of gleeful mischief. "Are you still desirous of owning Lightning?"

At the mention of the blood hunter, the earl eyed his sister with considerable intensity. "What are you at now, you devilish chit?"

"I'll wager Lightning that you cannot, within the space of one week, fix that young lady's attention to the point where she ignores that whelp."

The earl's expression turned dangerous. "Bess, you're not suggesting that I engage the woman's affections for a game? What kind of loose fish do you think me?"

"Oh! No, I see. You could not, nor would I want you to," his sister said quickly. "I only wager that you cannot persuade Rachel to be comfortable in your presence so that she enjoys your company."

"Now that I could do," Beresford agreed, mollified by his sister's explanation of her scheme. "You realize you will be giving up Lightning in a week?"

Elizabeth's eyes twinkled. "Only if you succeed. The Westfield ladies have a strange set of values."

He nodded energetically and then stood some moments in thought. Then suddenly breaking the silence, he turned to his sister.

"Why didn't you tell me situations like this arose during the season?"

Lady Elizabeth opened her mouth to disclaim any knowledge of such intricate problems, but looking out across the room with a new eye, Beresford had become attuned to the hopes and flirtations of the matchmaking society. He gave a sigh, crossed his arms and leaned one broad shoulder against the pilaster behind him.

"And hitherto, I had thought a mill or a race to be epitome of sport."

THE FOLLOWING DAY was fair, and Veronica had accompanied her auburn-haired sister on a quick shopping trip. They reached home in time to witness
Amabelle's tempestuous departure from the drawing
room. As the double doors slammed behind her, the
youngest Miss Westfield turned to see Veronica and
Rachel. She paused to favour them with a look of such
reproach that they stopped, frozen in the act of hand-
ing off their shawls and bonnets to a footman.

"And I hope it rains, spoiling all your enjoyment of
the evening!" she wailed.

Out of patience with Amabelle's tantrums, Veronica stripped off her gloves and gave her a smile as if she
had noticed nothing amiss.

"Nonsense, if the evening is ruined for us, it will not
avail you one whit. Be a dear and finish your tears before lunch, won't you? It will not do to cry in the tur-
tle soup. Too much salt ruins the delicacy of the
flavour."

Turned to hurl herself dramatically toward the
stairs, Amabelle was caught off stride by her sister's
amiable remark. Instead she gave Veronica the benefit of her most soulful expression.

"I don't expect understanding from you," she
moaned and flung one hand up to her forehead.

"I'm surprised you should, because your everlast-
ing tears are becoming a dreadful bore," Veronica
answered with a pleasant smile, as if she considered
her words as commonplace as a request for cream over
strawberries.

"But I do think we should take you to the theatre,
so you can view the new style in theatrics. Yours are

dreadfully out of date, you know." She took Rachel by the arm and firmly guided her into the drawing room before Rachel's sensibilities could override her surprise. Veronica hoped to shock Amabelle by making her see her vapours were gaining her nothing.

They entered the drawing room to find Lady Ellerbrook industriously composing a message while a footman stood by. Seeing her daughters, she rose, still holding the pen in one hand and an elegant gilt-edged paper in the other. Her face was alight with excitement as she started across the room.

"It is indeed good fortune that we had not committed ourselves for this evening..." she said, her words trailing off as she hurried back to finish her note.

Veronica and Rachel waited while their mama finished her note and gave it a twist. They were much surprised when Lady Ellerbrook named as the direction of this intended missive, Beresford House on Albemarle Street.

Veronica could not take it in good part when Rachel clasped her hands together and gave it as her hope that her mama had not engaged them to join any party containing Lord Beresford and Lady Elizabeth.

Heretofore, she had done what she could to ease her sister's discomfort, but this must be considered an excess of sensibility.

"Rachel, I wish you would give over this goosish behaviour," she announced with an asperity she made no attempt to hide. "What there is in Lord Beresford to which you take aversion, I cannot see."

Lady Ellerbrook raised one hand to her cheek, her blue eyes wide. Her gaze moved from one to the other in dismay. She sought to restore peace by pointing out an eligibility in Lord Beresford that must, to her, supersede most other considerations.

"Above thirty thousand pounds a year..." she faltered.

"He is quite unexceptionable." Rachel, too, had difficulty in speaking as she attempted to defend her feelings. "But both he and Lady Elizabeth are so quick-witted, I declare I feel most drab of mind in their presence. Surely I am only invited as a courtesy to the rest of you."

"Nonsense." Veronica saw this evening's invitation as an acquiescence to her request. Lord Beresford was making a push to fix his affections with Rachel. Still, she was not overjoyed that the invitation had come so quickly upon the heels of her suggestion. The feeling caused her some distress.

Yet, if a marriage contract came of her efforts, she and Charlotte would be able to continue their plans for Red Oaks School without interference. The solace she had expected to derive from those long-cherished plans eluded her.

SINCE BERESFORD HOUSE LACKED a hostess, the earl had named the entrance to the Vauxhall Gardens as the place for the gathering of his evening party. He and Lady Elizabeth were the first to arrive on the scene. They had hardly stepped down from the carriage when a second vehicle drew up, stopping a short distance away. Alighting from it was Lord Folkestone.

"I cannot believe the baron's presence is a coincidence," Lady Elizabeth said softly to her brother. "You are wicked indeed to serve Miss Westfield such a turn."

The earl gazed down his nose at his sister. "How not? If you think I will allow the insolence of females to go unchallenged, my girl, you are out."

And if Lady Elizabeth considered that warning to be for Miss Veronica Westfield alone, she was soon to learn of her error. A third carriage drew up and she was delighted to greet the portly gentleman with the snow-white hair and beaming smile, Squire Johns. She had known him since her childhood and valued him as a longtime friend of the family.

Her delight in seeing the squire was considerably lessened by the sight of his companion. She immediately recognized the short, slight figure of the Viscount Winsterfere who gazed around him with a look of disdain and boredom. His expression might have been an affectation at one time, but his face had now accepted it as a permanent mould. He was both the most persistent and the most annoying of those gentlemen who had formed Lady Elizabeth's court. While he energetically pressed his own suit, he had disparaged all the other gentlemen as fortune hunters.

Because for nearly a decade he had been pursuing any woman of wealth with a singular lack of success, his censure of his rivals was a joke shared by the earl and his sister. But finding Winsterfere had been invited to join the party for the evening was enough to bring a flash of fire to Lady Elizabeth's eyes. Her brother met it with a gaze of tranquil amusement.

"Careful how you go, my girl," the earl murmured under his breath. "You yourself have brought this about. You must know by now you cannot escape my revenge."

The three gentlemen were approaching, and while the earl was engaged in greeting Lord Folkestone, Squire Johns and Lord Winsterfere with the utmost affability, the four Westfield ladies arrived. Before the introductions had been completed, the Honourable Mr. Shavely had emerged upon the scene to even the number of gentlemen to escort the ladies and bring the party to ten.

Lord Beresford was just signalling to the dock man to provide the boats reserved for carrying the party across to the pavilion when he was interrupted by his sister calling a greeting.

"Dear Mr. Tonley, I'm so glad you could join us," she said as the young gentleman came through the entrance. Moving forward, Lady Elizabeth linked her arm companionably in his. "Do come and greet my brother who was just speaking of you this afternoon. He felt quite desolate that we see so little of you."

The earl's brow snapped down and his mouth drew into a tight line. To give the earl credit, he hid his irritation as he welcomed the self-effacing young man. Mr. Tonley stuttered his appreciation for being included in the party but appeared not at all gratified.

While Beresford paused to reconsider this new development, Lady Elizabeth stepped into the breach by leading Mr. Tonley over and requesting him to escort

Rachel aboard the boats that would convey them to the main part of the gardens.

"I-I would be m-most happy to," Mr. Tonley stammered, not quite able to meet the eyes of the young lady, but appearing quite surprised and pleased.

As Rachel murmured her delight at the arrangements, Lady Elizabeth continued to arrange the party to her satisfaction. She suggested Lord Winsterfere escort Charlotte and linked her own arm in that of Mr. Shavely. As Squire Johns had offered his arm to Lady Ellerbrook, both Folkestone and Beresford were left to accompany Veronica.

As the others moved away, Veronica raised her eyes to meet those of Lord Beresford, seeing in them a shared discontent. His frown deepened when Lady Elizabeth, departing on Mr. Shavely's arm, looked back at the earl with laughing eyes and wiggled her fingers in a fond farewell.

Veronica strolled between Lord Folkestone and the earl of Beresford, and was assisted aboard the third boat by the earl, who was taciturn and unsmiling.

As if to further exacerbate Veronica and Beresford's displeasure, the baron favoured them with a detailed account of his visit to a little-known bookstore, where he had come across the writings of one Reverend James Withewillow. From Folkestone's remarks, Veronica assumed she should have known the minister chronicled his travels in Africa and India. The worthy churchman seemed to have been bursting with solutions for bringing the light of Christianity to the heathen.

Well aware Lord Beresford was clenching his teeth to hold back some scathing remark, Veronica perversely encouraged the baron with interested nods and prompting questions. She ached to laugh at the earl's disgust. Her discomfort was alleviated only when they reached the opposite shore where Folkestone espied an elderly couple and excused himself to greet them.

"Lord," Beresford breathed when Folkestone was barely out of hearing, "much more of that and I may take refuge in the shrubbery—a good idea, that."

Taking Veronica's arm, he made an abrupt turn and took a small path that carried them immediately out of sight of the rest of the party. Baron Folkestone was still engaged in conversation with the couple, and had not seen them step from the most direct way. Veronica gazed up at Lord Beresford with a twinkle of mischief.

"My lord, that was not well done of you. I take it, since you arranged the party, you did invite the gentleman to join us?"

"I had not expected him to be in my company," Beresford said with some asperity.

A laugh escaped Veronica. "And who was to enjoy his company, my lord?"

The earl, overcoming his agitation, smiled wickedly down at her. "I assumed you had a partiality for his attentions." He spoke urbanely.

Veronica opened her mouth to protest when she saw the gleam of amusement in my lord's eye. "I see now how it goes," she murmured. "You expected from me the same liking for Lord Folkestone that Lady Elizabeth feels for Lord Winsterfere. I should be gratified to be elevated to the ranks of those in whose pleasure you take a somewhat irregular interest. I wonder what I have done to receive such consideration. Or—'' her glance turned equally wicked ''—how I might return such solicitous concern?''

Seeing he had been caught, the earl laughed softly. ''Do not think you can best me in my own game. If you plan to foist some ape leader on me, I warn you I won't stand for it!''

''I could not,'' Veronica said, this time seriously. ''That would interfere with my plans for Rachel. Doubtless your sister misunderstood; she has certainly cast a rub in the way.''

''She has done that,'' the earl said, his lips tightening.

They walked a few paces in silence, moving through the dimness of the deep twilight into pools of light as they passed the multicoloured lanterns that lit the path. Veronica was still irritated by the presence of the baron.

''You deserved Folkestone's prosing, you know. I cannot pity you.''

The earl gave her a long searching look, the expression in his eyes hidden by the shadows.

''Had it not occurred to you,'' he said, ''that in inviting the baron I was aiding not my own cause but that of your sister, Charlotte?''

''Charlotte?''

Lord Beresford pursed his lips and looked thoughtful. ''Surely you've noticed that she seeks his company? Would that be so if she had not developed some fondness for him?''

Veronica disagreed. "I cannot think even Charlotte could long be interested in such a bubble-head."

Beresford was not to be turned aside. "Reconsider. Your sister is by no means an antidote. I can only assume she's with the gentleman by choice."

The spectre of Charlotte forming a tendre for Lord Folkestone was enough to bring Veronica to an abrupt halt. "Oh, Lord!" she said, horrified at the very idea. "Should Charlotte marry that creature, I would spend the rest of my life hearing how he was improving his mind." The eyes she turned on the earl were wide with consternation. "You must be mistaken!"

"Mayhap," he said with tranquillity, "but to the eye of one who knows neither very well, they appear as much alike as the proverbial peas in the pod."

"They do," Veronica agreed in accents of utmost anguish.

"Moreover it's obvious," the earl ventured further, "that a great affection exists between you and your sister. Doubtless, she throws Lord Folkestone in your way in the hope that he'll win your approval of their alliance."

Veronica was distressed and shook her head dismally. "Better I should give Charlotte my support immediately and not be put through the agony of his constant prosing," she said, "though I shudder at the thought of having that man constantly in our lives."

"You could not be so bold," the earl objected. "She's a lady of sensibility. Imagine the mortification if he's not yet declared himself."

"I see," Veronica murmured, not sure she agreed with the earl's reasoning. Knowing she was not overly sensitive but having no wish to hurt Charlotte, she was willing to take advice.

"On no account should you mention the matter to her," the earl said, speaking with a great deal of authority.

"You may be right," she sighed. "But if I must not, there is nothing for it but to try to show an interest."

"I feel for you," the earl said. He raised his head and looked around with a hint of discontent. "We should join the others. I have bespoken dinner for this time."

With the solicitous attention reserved for the noble and the wealthy, the waiters and management had provided all that was necessary for a satisfactory repast. And though the dining box was large, the size of the earl of Beresford's party afforded a coziness that would have assured a convivial meal had the guests appreciated one another.

Lord Winsterfere monopolised Lady Ellerbrook's attention. Since she was a mother with four single daughters, he expounded on those attributes required by any young lady hopeful of a good marriage. He was apparently oblivious of the fact that his description of this imaginary ideal of all virtue, talent and fortune was unattainable by any one human being, or that he had reduced Lady Elizabeth and the three Westfield sisters to the veriest rags of eligibility.

Veronica immediately recognized Lord Winsterfere as one who, not being able to match the stature of those around him, was contenting himself with deprecation as a means of social levelling. Several times she was forced to cover her mouth with her napkin,

lest her smile betray her. Nor could she meet Lord
Beresford's eyes; his carefully veiled expressions
meant for her alone were fast throwing her into the
whoops.

But several others around the table, not so quick of
understanding, treated Lord Winsterfere and his theories with scorn. Squire Johns had been regaling
Charlotte with a lively but repetitious description of a
hunt. He broke off his story to expostulate with Winsterfere, but as he thought the ability to take a fence
and draw a covert far outweighed all else, his objections were not much heeded.

Lord Folkestone considered knowledge of Latin and
Greek far superior to being accomplished on an in-
strument or as an eligible hostess. His theories so revolted young Mr. Shavely that he broke off an
interesting discussion with Lady Elizabeth, for some
time centring on striped waistcoats, and hooted down
any suggestions that a proper wife might carry a tinge
of blue.

Veronica had been placing her attention on the earl.
His urbanity had slipped as he took in the differences
of personality and opinions. He had brought the unlikely group together with the sole purpose of teasing
Lady Elizabeth and Veronica without considering their
affect on one another.

Fortunately, before rising tempers resulted in embarrassment for the entire party, the covers were removed and Lord Beresford hastily suggested a turn
about the gardens before entering the pavilion.

When they left the box, Veronica remembered the
earl's ability to manoeuvre people as he wished, and

she was much interested in how he would order the party.

As he tried to lead Winsterfere toward Lady Elizabeth, she, too, proved that she expected the earl's manipulations and linked her arm through that of Squire Johns. In moving aside, she forced Shavely to step back, which placed him with Charlotte, to whom he offered his arm.

Moving forward, Rachel had nearly stepped into the path of the earl and Lord Winsterfere. In terror of both gentlemen, she hastily backed away and found herself in close proximity to Mr. Tonley.

Veronica suddenly realized that she must accept the company of the odious Lord Winsterfere, Baron Folkestone or the earl. The baron stepped forward and offered to escort her in the direction Lady Elizabeth and Squire Johns had taken. She reluctantly took his arm and strolled away from the rest of the group, feeling a most unladylike desire to commit violence upon three of the persons attending the gathering.

Her possible targets were Charlotte, because of her affection for the baron, the baron himself and Lord Beresford. Which would afford her the greatest satisfaction, she had not yet decided.

Seeing that they were being accompanied, Squire Johns raised his voice to gratify Veronica and the baron with a hunting tale. The timbre of his voice precluded any conversation between the second couple. At the first opportunity, Lord Folkestone guided Veronica down a smaller path and away from the country gentleman.

"Not all frivolities are limited to London society," he told Veronica in disparagement of the squire's interest. "How one can fritter away his time chasing a helpless animal is beyond my understanding."

Well aware of the damage that could be laid at the door of a family of foxes, Veronica was not wholly in agreement, but she chose not to elaborate. She would only give the baron an opportunity to continue his strictures. He prosed away on what he considered the responsibilities of those born to the upper classes.

Like the fox when harassed by the enemy, Veronica sought a means of escape. Twice that evening she had been privy to just such a venture, the first time when the earl wished to forgo the company of the baron, and most recently when the baron escaped the squire's hunting stories.

They were strolling through a veritable maze of paths separated by tall shrubbery. And when she saw a bench ahead, Veronica had the genesis of a plan. As they approached the seat, she began to limp and leaned on his arm.

"I declare I have a stone in my slipper," she said, wishing for a more original complaint but certain her excuse would fool the scholarly baron.

While he offered her his concerned attention, Veronica deliberately focused her eyes upon an intersection of paths deeper in the garden and then raised her gaze to the baron.

"Was I mistaken, or did your friends just pass down yonder path?" she asked, looking beyond him again.

At his look of confusion, she added, "I thought I saw the couple who engaged you in conversation when we first entered the gardens."

Folkestone brightened and turned to gaze in the direction of her gesture. More animation showed upon his features than had been apparent earlier that evening.

"The Reverend Ashton and his sister? Ah, if we could catch up with them I have every expectation you would find them most interesting," he said.

Veronica immediately arose as though she shared his enthusiasm, but when she took the first step away from the bench, she limped noticeably.

"That odious stone has bruised my foot," she said. "But if you hurried after them, perhaps I could rest while you brought them back...." She let her words trail away. The baron caught her meaning and nodded energetically.

"They were just crossing the intersection of the third path down," Veronica pointed out. "You could catch them with no difficulty."

At her assurance, the baron sketched her a quick bow, promised her he would return forthwith and hurried down the path.

Once he had turned the corner and disappeared behind a large hedge, Veronica rose from the bench and with not the slightest hint of a limp, hurried deeper into the maze until she chanced to find another secluded bench. She took a seat, opened her fan and fluttered it in some agitation. She must be fortified with some plausible excuse when once again she faced the baron. She was forming a quite credible story of limping after him and taking a wrong turn, when her heart leapt.

Lady Elizabeth was just passing the entrance to the nook. Veronica's spirits sank, thinking the viscountess and Squire Johns would insist on helping her to find her escort. It was not until the lady had almost passed, looked in and then most hurriedly sought the shelter herself, that Veronica realized the young widow was alone. She, too, appeared to be in the process of escaping dull company.

Veronica knew she could be misreading Lady Elizabeth's actions, so fanning herself in feigned agitation, she turned a serious gaze upon the newcomer.

"I have somehow become separated from Baron Folkestone," she said. "Have you by any chance seen him?"

"Had I seen that prosing bore, I would have crawled under a bush!" Lady Elizabeth answered with some asperity. "I myself have had enough trouble escaping the squire. Save being desirous of hiding myself from them, I've not given the others a thought."

Veronica settled back more comfortably. "Then we see eye to eye," she said with a smile. And folding the fan, she slipped the ribbon onto her wrist.

Lady Elizabeth sank onto the bench and patted the riband running through her pale gold curls. "What an abominable collection of gentlemen my brother chose to invite tonight."

This speech elicited a soft chuckle from Veronica and her eyes danced. "My understanding of the evening is somewhat muddled," she said.

"That is because you don't fully appreciate the devious mentality of your host," Lady Elizabeth retorted.

"I have a dim glimmer," Veronica countered. "For instance, it's clear to me that Lord Winsterfere was invited for your dubious edification—"

"And Lord Folkestone for yours," snapped the widow.

"Oh, no," Veronica contradicted. "Lord Beresford believes my sister has a tendre developing, and while I could have certainly done without his company, you must know your brother showed sensitivity in inviting the baron for Charlotte's sake...." Veronica paused as she noticed the suppressed smile on her companion's face. "Isn't it true? Did he have some other purpose?"

"I'm sure I don't know," Lady Elizabeth replied, not meeting Veronica's eyes. "If there is a feeling growing between them, then my brother has indeed shown sensitivity." She looked up to meet Veronica's gaze, her blue eyes shining with mischief. "I was thinking of your face when you saw Lord Folkestone was a member of the party."

"You believe he invited the baron because he knew I would be displeased at another lecture on sermons. Despite Charlotte's interest in the gentleman, I think you may be right." She frowned, counting on her fingers. "Winsterfere was to anger you, and Folkestone me, but who, pray tell, was Squire Johns to discomfit? Charlotte could not have given your brother any offence. Better he should have paired the gentleman with my mama."

Lady Elizabeth shook her head dismally. "That was his intention. We've known Squire Johns since our nursery days and a more interesting gentleman you might not meet. But since the death of his wife, he's turned his mind to hunting to the exclusion of all other interests. Even Julian had no idea the squire would be such a bore."

"Since your brother seemed so set on gathering the makings of a nightmare, I can hardly believe it," Veronica murmured.

Lady Elizabeth laughed. "Worse than he planned. In his attempt to run a rig on you and me, he has overstepped himself and even he cannot manage this unwieldy group. To give him credit, I don't think he expected to create quite such a mess."

"Pray, do not give him any credit," Veronica said crossly. "When I think of my poor mother, forced to listen to the views of that odious Winsterfere, I hope you will not take it amiss when I say I have the most unconscionable desire—"

"If you mean to do my brother bodily harm, put it out of your mind," Lady Elizabeth announced severely. "I am before you with a great number of grievances."

"Well and good if you do a thorough job of it," Veronica said darkly; her tone could have been construed as a threat. "But we are in a muddle. How can we leave our seclusion without chancing upon our escorts?"

"And I suppose we must leave it," the young widow sighed, looking around their inadequate shelter.

"I daresay we will soon find this bower a trifle confining."

"We must be careful how we tread," Lady Elizabeth said as she rose. They left the nook and walked slowly down the path until they reached the first intersection. They peered cautiously up and down before crossing. They had moved some distance across the gardens and were beginning to feel more at ease, when just after making a turn in the path, they heard hurried footsteps behind them.

"We're in the basket," Veronica said, turning anxious eyes on Lady Elizabeth.

But when they looked back, they found Charlotte hurrying toward them. They waited until the second Miss Westfield had joined them, her excuse already formed and ready to hand.

"This maze is most confusing," she said, "and it appears I have become separated from Mr. Shavely."

Appearing more diminutive than ever between the two tall Westfield ladies, Lady Elizabeth smiled up at Veronica. "I take it your sister has no overwhelming interest in gentlemen's waistcoats."

Though not given to humour, Charlotte was not slow of wit. Her narrow lips softened in a rueful smile. "I confess a gentleman whose total attention is on frippery does drive me nearly to distraction," she said.

"You are welcome to join us," Veronica told her sister. "However, no talk of fripperies, no fox-hunting, no—" She could not complain about Lord Folkestone. "Nor may you tell us of our shortcomings in the marriage mart."

"Done!" Charlotte said with a promptness unexpected from her stiff demeanour. "I daresay I will speak of flowers and stars and champagne. It does occur to me that I was in some erroneous expectation, believing that in a garden lit with coloured lanterns and moonlight there would be romance."

Never expecting such words to be uttered by her sister, Veronica gazed upon her in shock.

But Lady Elizabeth was already leading the way down a path not as brightly lit as many of the others. They rounded a turn and ahead saw a much travelled crossroads where a number of couples strolled by.

"I wonder if we should take the risk," Lady Elizabeth mused. "Surely our lost escorts would expect to find us on the more travelled paths."

"While making up our minds, we should step back a few paces," Veronica suggested. "We're standing in a pool of light."

Realizing their vulnerability, both Charlotte and Lady Elizabeth immediately moved back around the turn in the path. As the three ladies came to a stop, a voice out of the darkness considerably startled both Veronica and Charlotte and brought a squeak of fear from Lady Elizabeth.

"Oh dear..." the voice repeated.

From the shadows emerged the pale round face of Lady Ellerbrook. Veronica was not surprised. Escape was her mama's favourite means of avoiding anything she disliked. No doubt her tendency to do so had given her daughters the idea.

But once she had recognized the figure in the shrubbery, Lady Elizabeth accepted Lady Ellerbrook's defection from the company of her escort as the only sensible course.

"My lady, your brother has much to answer for," Veronica said decisively.

"I cannot think the earl—"

But Lady Ellerbrook was interrupted in her peace-making efforts by Lady Elizabeth, who announced without ceremony, "Pooh! If you cannot think Julian capable of putting everyone on the griddle to suit his purposes, you don't know my brother!"

"Well, I daresay..." Lady Ellerbrook's habitual expression of confusion became positive in her indignation. "If that isn't the most..." Not one to take offence when any other possibility presented itself, Lady Ellerbrook was unaccustomed to irritation. But the experiences of the evening brought out in her a response much akin to that of an angry rabbit.

Seeing her parent in such straits moved Veronica to give her shoulder a consoling pat.

"Have no fear, Mama. We will take revenge upon the earl. At the moment, the most pressing need is to find a pleasant place where we are both safe from prosing boredom and in tolerable comfort."

"This way," Lady Elizabeth said, brightening, as if she were just getting her direction. "If we head down this path we will be parallel to the long walk and will emerge at the temple."

Staying away from the main paths, the ladies soon reached that charming structure, well known to courting couples and those seeking quiet in the gardens. They discoveed a small nook overlooking an artificial lake. On the glassy surface were reflected the

lights of the coloured lanterns and the just rising
moon. They spent better than an hour in agreeable
conversation.

They compared modistes, hat makers, and Lady
Jersey's upcoming fête, to which they had all received
invitations. They were in high good humour when it
occurred to Charlotte that they had left Rachel un-
chaperoned. The irregularity of such a situation
brought Lady Ellerbrook immediately to her feet.
Veronica, however, was not at all alarmed.

"She is acceptably accompanied," she said comfortably. "She and Mr. Tonley will be at the concert.
They are both equally shy. The entertainment will have
prevented any need for conversation."

Lady Elizabeth rose from the bench. "If those shrill
notes I hear are from Haydn's *Tobias*, and my memory serves correctly, that is the last aria on the pro-
gram tonight."

Lady Elizabeth was quite right, and by the time the
four ladies had reached the entrance to the concert
hall, they found Mr. Tonley and Rachel leaving amid
a crowd of music lovers.

"Nothing else to do," said the viscountess, "we
must return to the box. Those trays passing along that
path herald the serving of supper."

"We'll tighten our stays and prepare to go easy over
rough ground." Veronica smiled mischievously at
Lady Elizabeth.

"Oh, do be quiet." Elizabeth flipped her fan. "If I
hear another word, I will see to it that the squire
bores on at you for the next week!"

They were just approaching the box as Lady Elizabeth laid this stricture on Veronica, who chuckled at her friend's reply.

When the ladies entered the box they did so with some trepidation, but they found themselves alone.

"Where are our charming escorts?" Lady Elizabeth asked, looking out over the walkway in front of the box.

"Out searching for us, I dare wager," Veronica replied with a smile.

The ladies took the seats at the rear of the box and waited. Shortly the missing gentlemen strolled into sight, led by a tight-lipped earl of Beresford.

Behind him, Squire Johns was lecturing the baron, whose expression of suffering showed his martyrdom, and following were Winsterfere and Shavely, in the midst of a heated sharp discussion overridden by the stentorian tones of the squire.

The earl stopped when he saw the ladies and Mr. Tonley at rest in the box. For a moment his attention was fixed on Lady Elizabeth, who wore an expression of sublime innocence. Then his gaze moved to Veronica, who chose momentarily to admit her part in the defection by giving him a triumphant smile.

When the other gentlemen noticed the presence of the ladies in the box, they came rushing over. Their questions and the replies of the ladies, who all claimed to be terribly upset about the separations, created a babble of confusion.

Behind them, and more important to Veronica, was the earl, who watched in forbidding silence.

The dark look he gave his sister and Veronica acknowledged their having emerged victorious in the evening's contest. His clenched jaw testified he had been the sufferer for having invited a set of boring gentlemen. But the turn of his mouth warned that they had best look to themselves.

He was declaring war.

CHAPTER FIVE

"IT IS QUITE an attractive hat," Veronica said. She was admiring the confection of straw and ribbons while the milliner stood to the side, hopeful of a sale to such tonnish young ladies.

Charlotte stood before the mirror and turned her head to view the effect. She might not be a beauty quite in Rachel's style, but Charlotte's delicate features could be brought out to advantage.

The bright pink and green ribbons added colour to the monotone of Charlotte's sandy-brown hair and eyes, but she shied away from anything she considered frivolous.

"I cannot think it in anything but the most common style," she said with some dissatisfaction. "But really it is quite a—gay—little concoction." And with those hesitant words she considerably surprised her older sister by resolutely tying the ribbons beneath her chin and nodding her acceptance to the shopkeeper.

When they had completed their purchases the two Misses Westfield left the milliner's shop and strolled up Bond Street.

"Veronica, will you cease that striding?" Charlotte demanded. "You walk like a countrywoman taking eggs to market!"

Veronica was not much discomposed by her sister's criticism, but she slowed and made an effort to shorten her steps as she smiled. "More than once I've carried eggs to market, and so have you."

"I beg you will not so blatantly advertise it!" Charlotte said. "Those unladylike strides are doubtless to blame for your being separated from Lord Folkestone last evening."

Since her sister's accusation was unjust, Veronica longed to express her dissatisfaction with the gentleman's company. But having given some consideration to what the earl of Beresford had suggested, she held her tongue and spared her sister's feelings. Instead, she gave Charlotte a mischievous smile.

"Do not, I beg of you, pull a Friday face on me. Mine was the legitimate case that gives a possibility of veracity to you, and to Lady Elizabeth and Mama."

"You would have done the same had you been forced to suffer the shallow-minded conversation of young Mr. Shavely," Charlotte snapped.

Veronica found the intricacies of society manners quite fascinating. Nor did she count the evening unsuccessful, for having escaped Lord Folkestone's prosing, her sense of adventure had been tickled by the remembrance of the four ladies lurking about in the gardens. Seeing the earl of Beresford caught in a trap of his own devising was a perfect capper on the evening.

Her only regret was that Rachel had not eschewed the company of Mr. Tonley and had been forced to endure that gentleman the entire evening. She said so to Charlotte.

"She might be as comfortable with him as any other," Charlotte replied. "In sharing the same discomforts they would not make the other's situation worse."

Thinking the matter over, Veronica could not be in agreement with her sister, but she chose not to pursue the matter, for Charlotte, never happy when shopping, appeared to be in a singularly dour mood.

They were approaching the shop of Madame Glisson when Veronica looked up to see Lord Beresford. She caught her breath as the gentleman came down the street. It was the first time she had been privileged to view him out of the social round. She was struck to find the nonchalance of his attitude when doing the pretty at a party was much different from the purposeful air with which he strolled down Bond Street.

His bearing and movement proclaimed the sportsman. The well-cut, blue bath-cloth coat, his neck cloth in the style of the Oriental, his fobs and quizzing glass were all those of a man of fashion. But there was about him an authority that caused those of lesser stature and social position to scuttle out of his path.

As his eye chanced to fall upon the Misses Westfield, he slowed his steps and doffed his curly-brimmed beaver hat. He offered them a smile of lazy amusement, but Veronica could see his expression had noticeably lightened. She thought he was in for a disappointment if he expected to find Rachel with them.

"Ah, my dear ladies," he said, "finding you alone, I must assume you have somehow misplaced your escorts again. Might I be of service?"

Behind his languid smile, Veronica could see the humorous intensity in his eye. Determined not to be caught by his wit, she looked suddenly about her before turning wide eyes back on the earl. "I do declare, sir, I feel you must be correct. What we can have done with the gentlemen I cannot at the moment explain."

Charlotte assumed Lord Beresford's raillery to be some aspersion on their conduct of the previous evening. Her mouth tightened perceptibly, but if Beresford noticed, he chose to ignore it.

"I am about an urgent errand for my sister," he said. "It seems she cannot last another day without a copy of Miss Radcliffe's new book. If you're heading in the direction of Hatchford's, I will endeavor not to lose you on the way."

If the earl had been trying to pacify Charlotte, he could not have chosen an invitation more fortunate than that of visiting the famous bookstore. She had looked forward to hours spent perusing the volumes, and had more than once complained that the exigencies of preparing for and taking part in the season had left her no leisure for visiting the most celebrated of literary marketplaces.

"We shall be in your debt, sir," Charlotte answered for both of them. Totally forgetting her purpose of finding a new walking dress, she lengthened her own steps to a stride as they approached and entered the bookshop.

Veronica left Charlotte gazing with prim rapture upon voluminous tomes of sermons and travel books and took herself off in search of other reading.

The earl found the book that had been his object and joined Veronica as she idly turned the pages of a slim volume of poetry. By its tattered condition it was far from new. As she put it aside, he picked it up and surveyed the title; his eyebrows rose and his light mood seemed to deepen.

"Now why," he mused, a plaintive note evident in his drawl, "don't I see you as one who would enjoy a lack of reality?" With that he laid aside the edition of light romantic poetry.

Veronica smiled back at him. "Would you expect me to be in raptures over Lord Byron? Is that still fashionable?"

It was in her mind to tell him that she had considered purchasing the small, worn volume for Rachel. Thinking he might not be overly fond of sentimentality, she chose not to mention it. Instead, she gazed about as if she felt herself at a loss in a strange place and then looked back at the earl with assumed helplessness.

"Mayhap, sir, you would like to point out something you think I would enjoy? I am persuaded you are far more familiar with Hatchford's than I."

The earl raised his quizzing glass, inspecting Veronica most carefully, a sparkle in his magnified eye. With a smile he turned and examined the shelves of books.

"Hmm, perhaps the writing of Simpson on Trafalgar? Since you seem to be most talented in strategic withdrawals—"

Veronica choked back a little laugh and gazed up at him with innocence much too feigned to be real.

"But perhaps I should think again," he said with pretended concentration. "You and my sister may consider that Trafalgar was child's play."

Veronica took a moment to look over her shoulder to assure herself Charlotte was not within hearing and then gave the earl the benefit of a mischievous smile.

"How could we do less, sir? I cannot think your guest list was for our enjoyment."

The earl's eyes twinkled. "Can you doubt it?"

"Well, in truth, I cannot. And you were justly served. But I fear the evening did not come out as you and I had planned. I found that disappointing."

"In what way?"

"In effecting a closer acquaintance between you and Rachel. I was under the impression your invitation was the result of our conversation the evening before."

"Was it?" The expression in his eyes was unreadable.

Veronica nodded, because it could hardly be otherwise.

"You can imagine my disappointment when young Tonley showed up on the scene. I daresay she was bored almost to the vapours."

"Well, don't lay his appearance at my door!" the earl said shortly. "I recognized the delicate hand of my sister there."

"Oh," Veronica murmured, as a sudden uncomfortable thought intruded. "It had not occurred to me that Lady Elizabeth might not be desirous of..." Her tongue stuck just short of saying that his sister might have other and more ambitious plans for her brother.

The idea that any other female could supersede Rachel in value kindled a spark in her eye.

Never behindhand in perception, the earl obviously read her change of mood and gave her another slow smile.

"I beg of you, don't tease yourself over Elizabeth's motives," he murmured. "Her plans and yours do not come into conflict." His gaze for a time centred on Veronica's face, shifted to look beyond her shoulder, and then back again. "Your sister is preparing to join you, so I'll leave you again. But think on this. My sister has her plans—and you have yours—but does it occur to either of you that I might have *mine*?" With another smile and a bow, Beresford turned and left the shop.

Gazing after him, Veronica knew his last words were a very thinly veiled challenge.

Charlotte had found several books she wished to add to the library at Red Oaks and was singularly animated and anxious to continue her shopping.

At Madame Glisson's she was giving only half a mind to her selections when, seeking to brighten her sister's wardrobe, Veronica attempted a bit of subterfuge.

"I declare this azure would not be my colour at all." She pointed to a fashionable walking dress lavishly trimmed on the cuffs and bottom of the skirt with violet braid. "I cannot for the life of me understand Lord Folkestone's preference for this colour."

Charlotte's voice turned sharp as she pushed aside some ribbon the dressmaker had brought out for her inspection. "I was not aware the baron was interested in female frippery!"

"Oh, I think he is not quite colour-blind," Veronica added, hoping to persuade her sister to more becoming styles and shades. "He appears to like tastefully bright colours." She fervently hoped her sister didn't attempt to verify her tale; it was wholly fabricated.

"I do not account the baron with one whit of knowledge about female apparel," Charlotte retorted with asperity. "But he is perfectly free to admire anything he wishes!"

Veronica was surprised. Had Charlotte and Lord Folkestone had some disagreement? Knowing her sister was not one to discuss a sensitive subject, she waited quietly while Charlotte finished her purchases and they prepared to leave the store.

Veronica noticed Charlotte had chosen to take the azure dress. She hoped this augured well for a reconciliation between the two scholars. And moreover, when the persuasive Madame Glisson insisted soft shades of blue and green were exactly the right colours to bring out Charlotte's delicate complexion, the prim-lipped young lady succumbed and made the purchase of three dresses.

They had just stepped onto the street when across the way they chanced to observe an unaccompanied young female. Her head was down and they were unable to see her face, but they recognized the blue sprig muslin and chip-straw hat with matching ribbons that only imperfectly concealed a head of guinea-gold curls. Their youngest sister was on Bond Street, unattended. Surprise caused their gazes to meet in startled inquiry, but neither Veronica nor Charlotte wasted time by asking questions of each other.

Dodging the passing carriages, they hurried to cross the pavement and come upon Amabelle. In order to avoid meeting a pair of curious women who were approaching her, Amabelle had paused and was peering into the doorway of a shop.

"There you are!" Veronica called, forcing a semblance of cheerfulness into her voice for the sake of the passersby. Though what good it would do, she could not imagine.

Surprised at the appearance of her sisters, Amabelle started, her guilt plain as she blushed crimson. "What—what are you doing here?" she stammered in confusion.

"Preventing you from entirely ruining all our reputations," Charlotte muttered as the two women passed out of hearing. "What could you be thinking of? Showing yourself so lacking in propriety as to—"

"Charlotte, cease!" Veronica's command cut into her sister's strictures as she saw, up the street, the slow procession of Mrs. Drummond Burrell's carriage. Accompanying her was the Princess Esterhazy. No two sets of eyes were sharper in detecting behaviour that smacked of the exceptionable.

"Amabelle!" Veronica ordered. "Rid yourself of that Friday face and smile!"

"Why?" Amabelle demanded, her mortification at being caught by her sisters magnified by Charlotte's remonstrances. She tossed her head in challenge. "So

you can put on airs while you shut me out of everything?''

"Then behave as you will," Veronica said promptly.
"Nothing will return us to Red Oaks faster than dis-
grace. Remember, neither Charlotte nor I wanted to
come to London."

Veronica's words acted powerfully upon Amabelle.
Her behaviour was nothing less than perfect when they
greeted the two hostesses of Almack's. Nor was she
given a chance to vent her feelings afterward, for they
had just stepped away from the carriage when they
were hailed by Lady Radley. She had finished her own
shopping and offered them a place in her carriage for
their return to Brook Street.

But in that short ride Amabelle had had time to
think over her circumstances and, while Veronica and
Charlotte paused to speak with the footman and ascertain their mama's whereabouts, she fled to her
room.

Veronica and Charlotte were not immediately able
to rid themselves of their feelings by confronting their
mother with Amabelle's behaviour since she was
lunching in Albemarle Street with a recently widowed
cousin.

So it was not until nearly tea time that Lady Ellerbrook returned to Brook Street, and by that time
Veronica's attention had been drawn to other matters. The afternoon post had brought a letter from
Oliver Pettigrew, the bailiff at Red Oaks. Veronica
spent a laborious afternoon writing a reply to Pettigrew as well as a note to John Hobart, the family solicitor.

When she joined the family for tea, Amabelle's earlier indiscretion was no longer foremost in her mind, but Charlotte had not forgotten it.

In hope of forestalling any anger from her mother, Amabelle had taken steps to put forward her side of the situation by writing a most impassioned note, much crossed out and underlined and blurred with falling tears.

She had, she insisted, accidentally become separated from the young Brentwood ladies, but Veronica and Charlotte did not believe her, and were using the incident to effect a return to Red Oaks. She was remaining in her room during tea as no young lady with any feelings could withstand the censorious looks she would be expected to suffer from her sisters.

"Well! I can only say this," Charlotte declared when her mother had finished reading the disjointed message. "We spent quite some ten minutes in speaking with Mrs. Drummond Burrell and Lady Radley. If the Brentwoods were present, *I* did not see them!" Charlotte turned a sharp eye to Veronica for confirmation.

"Nor did I," she said slowly.

"Well, I see just how it is," Lady Ellerbrook spoke up. "You wish to return to Red Oaks and any excuse will suffice...." Somewhat surprised with her own force of speech, Lady Ellerbrook let her words drift off, offering Veronica the opportunity to speak again.

"Returning home is not the answer," Veronica said. "In her present mood of imagined injuries Amabelle is as likely to destroy the reputation of the family there as well as in London."

"The poor child..." Lady Ellerbrook began, but even she could find no defence for Amabelle's behaviour, and let her objections die.

"The poor child should have remained at school," Veronica said, finishing for her mother on an unexpected note.

"I for one would like to know what prevented Martin from accompanying her," Charlotte commented.

"I cannot feel—I mean she is so sensible of being treated like an infant in leading strings—dear Amabelle can take some things so to heart...." Lady Ellerbrook fumbled for excuses until Veronica lost all patience.

"She threw a tantrum and you did not enforce the restriction, Mama," she said sternly. "But if she must behave as if she belonged in leading strings, she should be wearing them. Else her ungoverned activity will succeed in ruining all our chances. While you are considering her, give a thought to Charlotte and Rachel."

It was seldom that Veronica's tolerance was sufficiently overcome to cause her to speak out strongly against the activities of any member of the family. Lady Ellerbrook, Rachel and Charlotte gazed at her in some dismay.

Up to that time Rachel had taken no part in the discussion, but now she suddenly interrupted, her voice carrying an unaccustomed authority.

"Enough. We need time to consider. Nothing is better for clearing the mind than a brisk walk."

Though Rachel's peremptory contribution to the conversation did strike her sisters as somewhat unusual, they had, before gathering in the drawing room for tea, planned and dressed for a stroll. With little more ado, they gathered their reticules, tied on their bonnets and headed for Hyde Park by way of Charles Street. By unspoken agreement they left the argument and their anger in the drawing room.

They were just entering the park when the family was hailed by a familiar voice, one becoming increasingly odious to Veronica. They paused as Lord Folkestone hurried to join them.

He greeted all the ladies and turned to Veronica. "Was I mistaken or when I was in Hatchford's this morning did I not hear the clerk give a direction for an order of books to you?"

"To Charlotte!" Veronica said hastily, delighted she was able to turn his attention toward her sister. "She would be most pleased to tell you about them."

And while Lord Folkestone and Charlotte waxed eloquent on elevating literature, Veronica dropped back to walk with her mother and Rachel and discovered they had been joined by Mr. Tonley.

The stammering young gentleman offered Rachel his arm and they strolled down the path a little behind Folkestone and Charlotte. Veronica fell into step with her mother, casting dissatisfied glances at the park shrubbery.

"I declare, now they have learned to wait in the bushes," she muttered. "The next to pop out will be Lord Winsterfere!"

"Oh, do not say so!" Lady Ellerbrook quailed. She looked around in dismay. "I warn you, dear, if that gentleman were to join us—"

Veronica opened her mouth to speak, but for once her mother had determined to finish a sentence.

"—I will swoon away and have to be taken home by carriage!"

They had not gone many steps farther when a phaeton pulled by a pair of beautifully matched bays drew up beside them and they were greeted by Squire Johns and the earl of Beresford.

The squire had just purchased the spirited greys and was gratified by the admiration of Veronica, Rachel, and Lady Ellerbrook. Had he paraded his new acquisitions before all the members of the FHC, he would not have found experts to couch their comments more knowledgeably. The most unstinting praise came from Lady Ellerbrook. Her henwitted vagueness never extended to her love of horses.

Beaming at her, the squire ordered the earl of Beresford out of his seat with the ease of one who had known the nobleman since he was in leading strings. Squire Johns demanded the earl assist Lady Ellerbrook to enter the phaeton and judge the team as he put them through their paces.

At no time reluctant to admire a pair of high steppers, the dowager moved forward with unaccustomed alacrity. Lady Elizabeth might find the subject of hunting and blood animals boring in the extreme, but Veronica had no doubt her mother would enter into the subject with genuine enthusiasm.

Having greeted the earl and the squire, Lord Folkestone and Charlotte passed on to stop in the shade of
a tree and continue their rapturous discussion of the
sermons of one Bishop Lawley. Rachel and Mr. Tonley had effaced themselves and stood silently observ-
ing the other strollers and the passing carriages.
Veronica eyed her sisters' escorts and gave the earl of
Beresford the benefit of a most pained expression.

"Sir, I am convinced you are the bane of my family," Veronica said.

"I?" Beresford raised his quizzing glass and in-
spected her in shock. "Hold me excused, Miss Westfield. If you fault me for bringing Folkestone and
Tonley on the scene, you are much mistaken."

"You invited them last evening," Veronica accused, knowing full well he was not responsible for
Tonley even then, but she conveniently ignored this
one exception. "Now they feel they can usurp all our
time."

"It is apparent I must mend my ways," the earl replied with a meekness that brought a sharp look from
Veronica. "I can see I should be horsewhipped for allowing such travail to enter your life."

"If that was meant to win my sympathy, you are fair
and far off," Veronica retorted.

"Would I do any such thing?"

"My lord, there is little I would put past you."
Veronica threw a glance in his direction, and hastily
redirected her gaze lest he start her laughing.

"Why I don't eschew your company is beyond me,"
he complained. "You abuse me like a fishwife—or like
my sister."

"Since you may become my brother, why not?" Veronica asked.

"Why not, indeed?" the earl agreed, his gaze turning somewhat wary.

Engaged in watching her steps as they passed a rough place in the path, Veronica felt the silence lengthening. She glanced up, wondering if she had overstepped proper bounds. She was in time to see his bleak expression, and bit her lip, fearing she had given him hurt.

"Oh, do let us cry friends," she said impulsively. "I think it would be delightful always to look forward to seeing you."

"And for my part, I hope you will never lose that sentiment," Beresford answered, his eyes alight. Then once again he was the poised man about town, his tone warning Veronica he was about the mental arrangement of some rapper.

"But are we friends? You have an uncommon way of defaming my character," he complained. "I announced my intention to reform, and you offered me nothing but insult."

"You? Reform?" Veronica retorted. "I tell you, sir, I give no credit to that intention. You are still attempting your games. Witness my mother's riding even now with Squire Johns. I confess it puts me in the whoops."

"Why?"

"Because I am convinced you attempted to send me into a temper. But you are out there. She will enjoy it."

"Doesn't that prove I'm attempting to mend my ways?"

"It does not," Veronica answered, "only that you miscalculated."

The earl's expression was one of concerned thoughtfulness, belied only by the gleam showing through lowered lashes. "Then I wonder you do not do me some mischief," Beresford said.

"Which I promised you," Veronica said with high good humour. "But you must wait. Other matters have been taking my attention today and I need time for proper planning."

"Ahh, then I may still live in hourly dread that you will foist upon me some clinging antidote whose very presence will put me to the shudders—"

"No, I must find some other way of gaining my revenge. Though with the schedule of social engagements my mother has planned, I confess I have just not had the time to do the necessary thinking, plotting and scheming."

"No doubt you'll find the time," Beresford remarked, "and will make use of all available assistance. I cannot help but wonder what Charlotte would plan for me, since by her escape from Shavely last evening, she was as dissatisfied as you."

Veronica stifled a chuckle. "Perhaps I should enlist her aid. She would seek to mend your ways by trapping you in some secluded corner and reading to you from a volume of sermons."

"Good God! Then I hope you will not!" Beresford said in astonishment, apparently visualizing the episode taking place. "I beg of you, rather than Charlotte, seek the aid of Rachel or Lady Ellerbrook."

"Not Rachel, she is far too sensible of people's feelings and my mother would most certainly leave the task half done. No, I think if you object to Charlotte, my only recourse would be Lady Elizabeth."

"That won't do," Beresford declared and then seemed to think better of his objections. "Or perhaps it would. She is at present engaged in coming up with some scheme and should the two of you work together, at least I need expect only one assault."

"I find it inconvenient that a certain gentleman— just the person who could most imaginatively assist me—would probably not do so."

This remark brought a sharp look from the earl, who reached in a pocket and removed his snuffbox with deliberation. Veronica saw the action as stalling for time.

"Oh?" he said in a suddenly almost disinterested tone, as if the subject had begun to bore him. "And who, Miss Westfield, would he be?"

Her eyes sparkled as she looked up at him. "Why *you*, my lord. Who has proved himself more talented at spoking wheels than you yourself?"

Unaccountably the earl's good humour returned as he nodded thoughtfully. "Perhaps we could catalogue a few...." He paused, turned his head toward her with singularly tutorish expression and shook a finger close to her nose. "—Only a few, mind you, of my lesser triumphs to start you thinking."

"What sportsmanship, to help an adversary," Veronica replied.

"How not," he said, "for what is the game worth if your opponent is unarmed?"

But before they could continue the conversation, they were hailed from the carriage path where Squire Johns was just bringing the phaeton to a halt. The earl crossed the short distance to assist Lady Ellerbrook from the vehicle.

"Oh, such a lovely pair of high steppers I never..." Lady Ellerbrook began but lost her train of thought as she was helped from the carriage.

But while Veronica gave half an ear to her mother's disjointed conversation, she watched the earl. Instead of resuming his seat in the phaeton, he leaned over and spoke a few quiet words to the squire. That gentleman called to Mr. Tonley, asking him if he would care to take a turn and judge the horses' paces. With a stammered thank-you, Mr. Tonley returned the few yards down the path and took the seat beside the squire.

As the elderly gentleman gave the horses their office to start, Beresford directed a speaking look at Veronica and turned to Rachel.

"Miss Rachel, since you have been abandoned by your escort, may I offer you my arm?"

After a despairing look at Veronica, Rachel nodded and the party continued along the path. Veronica slowed her steps to allow some distance to develop between the pairs of walkers and half listened to Lady Ellerbrook's continued praise of the squire's new cattle.

Normally Veronica was interested in horses, but she soon had a surfeit of knowledge about those particular creatures. Her gaze kept returning to the couple in front of her. By the movement of the earl's head, she could tell he was carrying the burden of the conversation.

But Rachel's bonnet absorbed most of Veronica's attention. Rachel had begun her walk with the earl with her head lowered in painful shyness. Following with her mother, Veronica could not even see the raised brim over the crown. As the walk progressed, a mere fraction of the brim became visible. Then more of the flower-trimmed confection came into view. Rachel was becoming more interested in the monologue of the earl, and before long, Veronica was treated to her sister's profile as she tilted her face to gaze up at Lord Beresford and return some comment.

With the lifting of that brim, Veronica's own spirits fell. She suddenly lacked any interest in viewing society out for a stroll. She felt the change in her mood, and searched for a reason.

She settled it in her mind that an afternoon walk in Hyde Park was far too public for her taste. She much preferred the paths around Red Oaks. She would be glad to return home. Her thoughts were forced and deliberate, bringing with them the feeling of discomfort usually associated with a lack of honesty.

Nor was her mood lightened when they returned to Brook Street. Lady Ellerbrook had stopped in the drawing room, so it was the three sisters whom Martin confronted in the upper hall. She informed them that Amabelle had left the house almost as soon as they and had been espied by that worthy servant going to the Brentwood house next door. In her capacity as a long-term servant of the Westfield family, Martin was known for direct speech upon occasion.

"And I will tell you the truth, Miss Veronica," she said, speaking to the eldest Miss Westfield as though she were head of the family, "that the talk about Miss Brentwood is such that I cannot feel easy having that child in her company."

Most of the family were accustomed to deferring to Veronica for levelheaded action. Charlotte turned to her eldest sister, prim-lipped with disapproval, and implored her to do something about Amabelle's behaviour.

"And for my part," she said, adjusting her bonnet as though she was ready to back words with action, "I do not think it would come amiss to walk up to that door and demand her return home!"

"Oh, but you could not do so," Rachel urged, her eyes large with concern. "How mortifying it must be for Amabelle."

Veronica rounded on her sensitive sister with unaccustomed ill-humour.

"Rachel!" she snapped. "It is one thing to care about people's feelings and quite another to allow your sensitivity to turn you into a perfect goose." She turned on her heel and marched into her room, closing the door with far more force than was necessary.

Once alone, she removed her bonnet and tossed it on the small writing table together with her reticule and gloves. Not caring if she wrinkled the new walking dress, she threw herself back on the bed and stared up at the rococo trim on the ceiling. She lay there, heartily wishing Cousin Henry had lived another fifty years. Her desire for her cousin's continued life stemmed less from affection than from the trouble the inheritance had brought into her life.

She would return to Red Oaks immediately, with or without the family. But even as she thought of it, she knew she would not carry out that plan of action.

Now that he had broken through Rachel's shyness, the earl of Beresford would see what a lovely young lady she was and would certainly make her an offer. Veronica hoped he would move speedily so they could return to Red Oaks before Amabelle created more difficulties.

But she could not understand her own feelings, for, with the exception of her youngest sister's recalcitrance, her plans were moving forward more speedily than she could have hoped. Actually very little time had been lost in attracting an eligible suitor for her sister's hand and in setting the courtship in motion.

But Red Oaks seemed so far away it could have been in another world. The plans for the school, which had taken her time and attention for years, seemed to be from a half-forgotten time. She tried to concentrate on the dear old manor house and her dreams for it, but intruding into the vision was the well-shaped head and rugged features of the earl of Beresford, his eyes crinkling with laughter.

CHAPTER SIX

THAT EVENING THE WESTFIELDS attended the Cavendish ball. It would be accounted the social success of the season, but Veronica found it wanting.

She had arrived at the ball with several audacious and unworkable plans for her revenge upon the earl of Beresford. Her intention had been not to carry them out, but to lay them before him as suggested revenge. Lacking in guile, she did not realize she was simply planning to keep their lighthearted conversations going because she enjoyed his company. Nor did she recognize her feelings as disappointment when, instead of devoting any time to their humorous sparring, he led Rachel on the floor, not once, but twice. Furthermore, he was before Mr. Tonley in inviting Rachel to join him for supper.

Because of the crush, Veronica had had little difficulty in avoiding Lord Folkestone, who arrived late and did not discover the Westfields until the evening was nearly spent. Deprived both of the necessity for dodging the prosing scholar and of the earl's company, Veronica felt the evening altogether dull.

Nor was she at all happy to see Charlotte becoming so enamoured of the baron. His fustian disposition was working powerfully on Charlotte. It was too bad of her to drive her family into frustration with her disdain of the frivolous, but for her to display such an attitude in public would be ruinous.

The next afternoon Veronica, Charlotte and Rachel were taking tea with Lady Radley, who had invited several society women for the unexpressed but very real purpose of gathering and trading all the latest gossip.

While Veronica sat holding her cup and listening to the vivacious talk, she overheard Mrs. Loomis, a vitriolic matron who was bringing out two butter-toothed daughters with a pronounced lack of success. She was talking to Charlotte. Before long the matron was commiserating with Charlotte for her ill fortune in being in residence so close to the Brentwoods.

"I cannot think what Clara Brentwood is about to let that girl ruin herself. She has not been given vouchers for Almack's," Mrs. Loomis was saying. "Elsa is entirely too fast, encouraging every raff and scaff in the Life Guard. Now I hear she's dragging her young sisters into the affair. I'd not have my daughters in their company."

"Most admirable sentiments," Charlotte replied tranquilly, "for there are so many better places one can drag one's unmarried daughters."

Veronica stifled a chuckle as she heard Mrs. Loomis's furious gasp. But Charlotte was not slow to bring up the subject as they made the short walk from Audley to Brook Street. The outrage Charlotte had withheld from Mrs. Loomis, she visited upon Veronica.

"If we are going to emerge from the season's activities with our heads up, you might consider making less of a push on your wardrobe and a little more in guiding Amabelle,'' Charlotte snapped at Veronica. "And I hardly think the garments you're affecting in London will inspire confidence in the parents of the students of Red Oaks. That is, if you have not given up the idea of the school entirely.''

Veronica was about to answer, but Rachel, feeling it incumbent on her to defend her sister, placed a calming hand on Charlotte's shoulder.

"It cannot all be laid at Veronica's door...'' she reasoned.

"Oh, I do like that term—not all,'' Veronica snapped, rounding on Rachel. "If you have attempted to exercise any influence on Amabelle, I've been completely unaware of it.''

This remark sufficed to bring tears to Rachel's eyes and recall Veronica to a sense of propriety. Angry as she might be, she had no cause to take her feelings out on Rachel. The sisters tactfully maintained silence until they arrived at Brook Street and retired to their separate rooms.

But once she had removed her hat, Veronica recalled that she had, earlier that morning, begun a somewhat lengthy letter to John Hobart. Turning her mind to business might help calm her spirits, she decided. She had left the unfinished missive in the escritoire in the back drawing room. Her first thought was to send a footman for it but, too impatient to wait, she determined to go herself.

She was in the hall and just passing Amabelle's room when she heard strident voices.

"You are not my mother and I don't have to listen to you!" Amabelle shrilled with anger.

Charlotte's voice, cool to the point of iciness, was lower pitched but came clearly through the door, which stood slightly ajar.

"That young female has made herself the talk of the town," Charlotte was saying, "and if you continue being seen in the company of the Brentwoods, your reputation will be no better than theirs."

"That's not true," Amabelle wailed.

"You cannot associate with people of ill-breeding and be accepted in the right society when you make your own come-out. If you think otherwise, you are sadly mistaken!" Charlotte persisted.

Veronica paused and stood weighing the advantages of leaving Charlotte to try to bring Amabelle to her senses against entering the room and attempting to calm sorely tried tempers. Behind her she heard a faint rustle. Turning her head, she saw her mother.

Lady Ellerbrook's eyes had taken on a intense awareness and her lips folded in a severity much akin to Charlotte's habitual expression. She stepped around Veronica and threw open the door. "Who is being talked about?" she demanded with no preamble.

Charlotte gave her mother a full accounting of the tales that had reached their ears and added, "I make no judgment on Elsa Brentwood, but consider, Mama, while a person may have nothing to do with the whitewashing of a wall, if she should brush against it while it's wet she is marked by it."

Veronica could not but admire Charlotte's choice of metaphor. It was doubtful that anything could have brought the circumstances home to their mother more forcefully, and by her expression she was most struck.

Not one to go against her youngest daughter's tantrums without trepidation, Lady Ellerbrook took a deep breath. "My dear," she said hesitantly, "I do fear we must heed what Charlotte is saying."

"Oh, you will not!" Amabelle broke in, tears flowing copiously. "It is beyond anything reasonable that I must give up my friends because Charlotte has taken them in dislike."

"But if they're giving themselves the name—"

"They're not!" Amabelle insisted, her eyes flashing. "If there is talk about them, it's Charlotte's doing. Because she does not wish me to do anything but read dusty old books and teach in that horrid school!"

"Now that's unjust," Veronica asserted. She stepped briskly into the room. "I also overheard the talk."

But Lady Ellerbrook was no longer listening. Amabelle had been most astute in mentioning the plans for the school. Their parent had long deplored her daughters' desire to begin a business enterprise. She accounted any mention of the scheme a threat to her hopes, more serious than anything her youngest daughter was likely to do.

"I have heard nothing to make me believe Miss Brentwood..." Lady Ellerbrook murmured, careful not to meet the eyes of her two disapproving daughters.

"Mama, they're making it up," Amabelle insisted. "They wanted me to stay at that horrid seminary of

Miss Filibrew's, and because you allowed me to come to town with you, they are trying to make my life miserable!"

"I cannot think Charlotte or Veronica would..." Lady Ellerbrook floundered. Then, with the dexterity of one who made a habit of escaping difficult situations rather than dealing with them, she noted the time and, insisting she must dress, she hurriedly escaped the room.

Veronica and Charlotte traded resigned glances and returned to their own rooms. Amabelle would continue her tirade as long as she was provided with an audience. Left alone, her usual buoyant spirits would take over. And while she might plot and scheme to find a way out of her dilemma, Amabelle was not one to stay in misery.

Lady Ellerbrook had indeed been shaken by the disclosures of Charlotte and Veronica, so much so that she announced her intention of sending her regrets to the Countess Gulsey, to whom they were promised that evening for a ball. She sent a hasty note around to Lady Radley, asking her to escort the three Misses Westfield in Lady Ellerbrook's stead.

"Which will most likely undo the good of this afternoon's altercation," Charlotte surmised as they passed from room to glittering room at Gulsey House.

Veronica nodded, forced to agree with her sister. "I think Mama was ready to insist Martin accompany Amabelle."

"Sooner or later, even she must see the necessity," Charlotte remarked.

"I think she has done so, but Amabelle will have talked her out of it before we hear the notes of the first dance," Veronica said.

"Oh, I cannot think she will," Rachel objected. "According to what Martin overheard, Mama seemed quite set in her mind that something must be done."

Veronica cast an irritated glance at Rachel and wondered how she could ever have considered Rachel's sweetness as anything but cloying. She bit back her sharp answer as she saw the earl of Beresford approaching, moving with more speed than his usual nonchalance allowed. Glancing just beyond him, Veronica saw the reason in the person of Mr. Tonley, who was also heading toward the three Misses Westfield.

Obviously the earl knew of the approach of his rival, for he bowed to the young ladies, gave Veronica a conspiratorial look and immediately requested the company of Rachel in the *rolande*, which was just forming.

Rachel shyly accepted the invitation and laid her hand upon the earl's proffered arm. Her face paled as she looked up to see Mr. Tonley joining the group.

That young gentleman had crossed the room with purposeful strides, his every movement pronouncing him on the way to request the company of a lady in the dance. Veronica eased back behind Charlotte so it was the latter who received his invitation.

As the two couples took to the floor Veronica stood watching. Less than a week before, she would have thoroughly enjoyed watching the earl's machinations, but now she was finding them depressing. Recalling herself to a sense of propriety, she glanced around the room to locate Lady Radley; though it was quite permissible for the three Westfield sisters to be together without a chaperon, for her to be alone for any length of time must cause stares.

Not readily locating the baroness, she walked down the room just in time to see a flip of pale blue silk disappearing into an alcove. Recognizing that particular shade as one worn by Lady Elizabeth that evening, she turned her steps in that direction. Veronica peered into the small chamber to find the young widow fanning herself in some agitation.

After assuring herself that no one was close enough to be within hearing outside the door, Veronica stepped in so that she was hidden from the vision of the other guests. Without ado she asked, "Winsterfere or Squire Johns?"

Those two names caused Lady Elizabeth to whirl around, her face the picture of extreme alarm. But seeing Veronica she sighed with considerable relief and snapped the fan closed.

"Winsterfere!" she hissed, one slipper-shod foot stamping silently on the Savonnerie carpet. "I declare I must do something perfectly horrid to Julian, for he's encouraging that dreadful creature. Mayhap we could put our heads together and take a beautiful revenge."

Veronica smiled and shook her head sadly. "This time I must cry craven," she said. "At least for the present. I do agree he can be most annoying but he is showing determined attention to Rachel."

At that remark, Lady Elizabeth's lips tightened. Her nod was sharp and abrupt as she flipped open her fan again and fluttered it vigorously.

"I've taken notice of that particular idiocy."

Pride in Rachel and in unnumbered generations of Westfields stiffened Veronica. From her height she looked down on the diminutive viscountess, her own face rigid with insult. Lady Elizabeth immediately realized how Veronica had taken her judgment of the situation.

"Don't go starched and pompous on me," she said to Veronica, her smile mischievous. "I've no objection to Rachel, but it won't do, you know."

"Why?" Veronica's voice still carried a residue of stiffness.

"He frightens her witless, and her sweet, amiable nature would bore him to death in a month. And, I am persuaded, *you* would be miserable."

"I?" Veronica's anger was lost in astonishment. "Why would I be miserable? Seeing Rachel happily married is one of my fondest wishes. If she should make an eligible connection, the circumstances would allow me to continue my plans unfettered by my mother's objections. At least I am persuaded such would be the case."

"Stuff!" Lady Elizabeth ejaculated. "Your fondest wish is Beresford."

So bald a statement left Veronica totally bereft of words and she sank on the small sofa, struggling to get her thoughts in order. "I fear, my lady, you don't understand my plans. For years, my sister and I—"

"Oh, I know all about that school. A more skip-brained notion I've never heard," Lady Elizabeth retorted. "Particularly with things going along so swimmingly between you and Julian, Charlotte and her odious baron, and Rachel with her stammering Tonley."

"Oh, no. It's not that way at all," Veronica objected, her head swimming from Lady Elizabeth's terse assessment of the situation. "I daresay Rachel, with her delicate sensibilities, merely sees in Mr. Tonley someone who needs her support. She is a most caring person. And Charlotte's interest in Lord Folkestone..."

"The intention she expresses to herself is to match you with that gentleman," Lady Elizabeth said. "Why do you think she keeps flinging him at your head at every conceivable opportunity?"

"Oh, no! She could not have any such purpose in mind," Veronica insisted, totally revolted at the idea of an alliance with Folkestone. "No! I am persuaded her association with the baron is due to her own personal fondness for him."

"Most assuredly," Lady Elizabeth agreed as if there could be no doubt in the matter. "You will not say of your sister that she would wish to do you any injury?"

"She'd never consider such a thing."

"Or that she would want anything for you but what she considered the very best."

"Charlotte would always want the best for me," Veronica assured Lady Elizabeth.

At which point that lady dimpled prettily, snapped her fan closed again and used it as a wand to point at Miss Westfield. "Exactly! And what standard would she use for choosing the best?"

"Well—what *she* thought held the most value." Veronica was hesitant, unsure where the conversation was leading; she was afraid to continue it and too fascinated to ignore it. Her pulses were pounding with dread and anticipation. She dimly understood where Lady Elizabeth was heading, but when she tried to send her own mind along that path, it turned stubborn and balked. She hoped the young widow's estimation might show the situation to be less than she feared.

"She'd use her own judgment." Lady Elizabeth smiled. "And what greater compliment could she pay you than choosing a gentleman she would want for herself?"

"As you say, she would choose for me what she most admired," Veronica said, her voice a bit weak and breathless. The viscountess was pointing out what Veronica had not wanted to face. Miss Westfield, who had bested solicitors, recalcitrant workers and spirited, half-trained horses, wanted to gather her skirts and run from the pretty little woman on the sofa.

"And how did you go about choosing a husband for Rachel?" Lady Elizabeth pressed on, her eyes alight with humour.

"Well, I—er—I'd certainly try to find a gentleman who—who..."

"Who appeared to be ideal—by *your* standards. In short, Beresford."

"Oh, no, I wouldn't do that to Rachel, or to myself." Even as she spoke, Veronica knew she had done exactly what she was denying. She turned stricken eyes on Lady Elizabeth; the situation was too dire for her to appreciate the sparkle in her companion's eye and she looked away. There was certainly nothing to laugh at.

Charlotte had committed herself to arranging a marriage for Veronica with a gentleman for whom she was feeling a growing tendre, and Veronica had done the same for Rachel. How had they got themselves into such a tangle?

"Now, you've denied all this, so it may be that you don't see..." Lady Elizabeth said.

But Veronica shook her head miserably. "Only a stupid person refuses the truth." She thought back to Charlotte's increasing ill humour at her and the way she herself had snapped at Rachel. She now recognized the irritation as jealousy, both in Charlotte and herself. But what was she to do?

Unable to sit still any longer, she rose and paced back and forth. And as she neared the door to the small withdrawing room, she caught sight of Lord Beresford leading Rachel toward the supper room.

Rachel's cheeks were pink and flushed from the efforts of the dance, and the movement of her head showed she was in easy conversation. She had indeed lost her shyness with Lord Beresford.

Veronica turned away from the door. What could she do?

Nothing.

It was already too late.

CHAPTER SEVEN

VERONICA'S NIGHT had been restless. Her illuminating talk with Lady Elizabeth at Countess Gulsey's ball kept running through her head. When she awoke and raised herself to accept a morning chocolate, her head pounded until she felt dizzy. For the first time in her life, Veronica succumbed to a servant's coddling and allowed herself to be dosed back to sleep.

It was therefore midafternoon when she finally rose from her bed. She felt heavy and listless, the aftermath of the medication, but with the clear knowledge that she must make an effort to straighten out their tangled lives. She had barely finished dressing when Charlotte tapped at the door and entered the room.

"Are you sure you should be up?" Charlotte asked, eyeing her sister with some concern. "When you succumb to remaining in bed, I confess you put me to the worry. You were never ill at home."

"Staying at Red Oaks might have prevented my problem; returning could not now solve it," Veronica said. "Will you join me for a walk? I have a great wish to be private with you."

Nothing loath, Charlotte nodded readily. Since the day was fair and several people were on the street, the Westfield ladies set their direction for Hyde Park and moved as fast as the greeting of acquaintances would allow. But once in the park at an unfashionable hour of the day, they were alone. Charlotte opened the conversation.

"You were quite right in suspecting Amabelle would succeed in changing Mama's mind."

But Veronica was not at that moment interested in her younger sister and waved the subject away with an imperious hand.

"What I wish to discuss is of far more import."

Charlotte was not pleased to have Veronica so cavalierly dismiss her major concern. She gave the strings of her bonnet an irritated jerk.

"If you can think of any subject more important than that silly chit's thoughtlessness, I'd like to hear it," Charlotte said.

"Our future happiness," Veronica stated flatly. "We can bring Amabelle to heel if we make up our minds to do so. But you and I have created a tangle far worse—and far less easy to correct."

"We have?" Charlotte said in startled accents. "I fear your dresser may have given you more than the proper amount of tisane."

"She hasn't," Veronica said. "When I'm finished, you will see for yourself." With that she related almost word for word her conversation with Lady Elizabeth the evening before.

But though she did not pooh-pooh the situation as impossible, Charlotte was totally unconvinced.

"But you will not deny," Veronica countered, "that you have been trying to bring about an alliance between Lord Folkestone and me."

"I would be a goose to do so under the circumstances," Charlotte admitted, considerably displeased at having her plans so easily discovered. "Nor can I be faulted. You will admit he is a gentleman of most elevated mind, most astute, and...studious."

"I will admit he had a most admirable character," Veronica said hastily, wanting to bring Charlotte's list of his virtues to an end. She did not succeed; her sister was caught up in her subject.

"And moreover, his sensibility to what is correct and just would never lead him to the excesses of gambling...." Charlotte continued to praise him until Veronica interrupted with some compliments of her own.

"And moreover, I am comfortable with the idea that no family could view with anything less than pride a connection with such an august name." Veronica felt it incumbent upon her to add some praise herself since her next words must be unwelcome to her sister. "But while I cannot but be aware of all the fine attributes the baron possesses, you must consider, Charlotte, I am not at all scholarly and my graceless levity would drive him to distraction."

"It would not hurt you to be a bit more circumspect in your thinking," Charlotte said by way of chastisement.

"Most assuredly," Veronica said. "But we are not now speaking of my deficiencies of character, but of the difficulties we've made. I am in exactly the same case as you. Let us for the moment consider the choice I have made for Rachel. You must agree I have chosen a gentleman of superior looks and birth whose fortune, I understand, is quite large.''

''Those are not proper considerations for happiness,'' Charlotte remarked.

''No,'' Veronica agreed. ''Nor when my eye first lit on the earl of Beresford did I know any of those things. What attracted me to the gentleman in the original case, was his pleasant attitude in teasing Lady Elizabeth, his sense of humour and the liveliness of his mind.''

''None of which will weigh strongly with Rachel,'' Charlotte surmised. ''Indeed if I understand her correctly, she is in dread of the earl's sharp wit. He would drive any female into nervous spasms within a fortnight.''

''Not any female,'' Veronica remarked. ''And you cannot deny he would make for a lively life.''

It was Charlotte's turn to give an exasperated and worried sigh. She was silent for a moment and then lowered her head, capitulating. ''It appears we have created a pickle of a situation.''

''Part of it can be easily handled,'' Veronica said and took Charlotte's hand in both of hers. ''I also know you have been acting out of your genuine concern for me, but the baron would not suit me at all. You may be easy on that head.''

Charlotte nodded thoughtfully. ''Now that we have spoken frankly, I feel much better. I've been extremely difficult to live with these past few days, but I could not—would not find the reason for myself.''

"And I've been unfair to Rachel." Veronica made her own admission, glad she was able to say it, and so release part of her guilt.

They walked for some moments in silence, and then with unaccustomed tenderness, Charlotte took Veronica's arm.

"I am persuaded the situation cannot be as hopeless as you think. I will not believe the earl of Beresford could interest Rachel."

Veronica turned away to continue the walk, not wanting even Charlotte to see the pain in her eyes. "Then you did not see Rachel laughing up at him during supper at the Gulseys' last evening," she said. "I fear the charm that captured my heart has now taken hers."

The path Veronica and Charlotte had taken wound among the trees and flowering shrubbery and intersected the carriageway of the park.

They were just approaching the drive when a smart barouche came in sight. The coachman kept the pair of high steppers under strict control while the single occupant looked about her. When she tilted her parasol, the Misses Westfield recognized Lady Elizabeth at the same time she saw them. The carriage came to a halt and the lady waved urgently.

"If we haven't enough on our minds, we must now be interrupted with foolishness," Charlotte complained.

"Charlotte," Veronica snapped, "I beg you will not drive away the only person who has a mind quick enough to be of assistance to us."

They increased their pace as they approached the carriage, where the young widow waited, her eyes sparkling with the liveliness with which Veronica had credited her, but her first words were not indicative of any serious thought.

"I am so glad I found you. I find myself in the midst of an odiously dull afternoon. Would you please come and have tea with me?"

"We're honoured by the invitation, but I believe Mama is expecting us to return to Brook Street—" Charlotte began a well-mannered excuse, but Veronica interrupted her.

"But if Lady Elizabeth will allow one of her servants to take a message, I'm sure Mama can do without us this one afternoon." Veronica could not read the message in the widow's eyes, but she was aware of her speaking look.

Charlotte gave no answer, but as Lady Elizabeth opened the door to the carriage, she stepped in, taking a seat with her back to the driver. Veronica followed, sitting beside Lady Elizabeth, and the coachmen put the horses to.

Lady Elizabeth leaned back in the seat and sighed. "I declare, I was surprised to see Lord Fernthisly last evening. I had heard he was in ill health, and he certainly looked it."

Charlotte looked blank and vouchsafed no answer. Veronica could not put a face to the name.

"I think we did not meet the gentleman."

"Just as well. In strictest confidence..." Lady Elizabeth proceeded to favour the Westfield sisters with a stream of gossip about people they knew only slightly. Her discourse lacked the spice of genuine scandal, but sounded as light-minded as any of the hostesses of the ton. She continued nonstop until they had reached Ivors House on Albemarle Street. After she had sent a message to Lady Ellerbrook, she led her guests to the drawing room.

Once she had ordered tea, Lady Elizabeth turned to her guests.

"Enough of commonplaces, what are we going to do about this muddle?"

Veronica had informed Charlotte of Lady Elizabeth's masterful reading of their situation, but to have it brought up so sharply caused her to draw back. She folded both her hands and her lips, taking a forced breath before she spoke.

"I'm afraid I don't understand you," she said, her voice cool.

"You have some plan?" Veronica asked, overriding Charlotte's reserve. She turned to her sister. "With Beresford for a brother, you must know Lady Elizabeth is accomplished in devious thinking." She cast a startled eye on her hostess. "I hope you will not take that amiss."

"Certainly not." Lady Elizabeth looked pleased, then her mouth drooped. "I haven't a plan, but I thought the three of us might concoct something excessively brilliant."

Veronica was disappointed, but not dejected. "We might, if we put our minds to it."

"I cannot think that I will be much help," Charlotte said. "My mind does not run to machinations."

She admitted the defect with more than ordinary pride.

"Exactly," Lady Elizabeth said. "But I am often led into flights of fancy, and even Miss Westfield must admit to having made a mull of it. We will conjure means, and depend upon your levelheadedness to call us to book if, in our enthusiasm, we step beyond the line."

Had Lady Elizabeth tried, she could not have countered Charlotte's objection with an answer more calculated to win the support of that prim young lady.

Charlotte nodded, her face softening. "I cannot think, even in your wildest thoughts, that either you or my sister would consider anything unseemingly. But you may depend upon my assistance."

"Then between the three of us, we will soon have a remarkable plan," Veronica said, smiling on the other two.

Once the alliance was formed, the three young ladies sat staring at one another. Charlotte remained stiff but expectant, her hands folded in her lap. Veronica searched the other two faces, and finding no help, busied herself smoothing the ribands on her reticule. Lady Elizabeth alternately smiled and frowned, twisted a curl and shifted her position on the *confidante*. They did not have an idea between them.

Charlotte broke the silence. "Mayhap we should consider what ingredients we have in this stew. By considering them one at a time, we might discover an idea."

"The first thing I want to do is separate Beresford and Rachel," Lady Elizabeth said with some force. "I tell you as I have your sister; the alliance could never be a happy one."

"I agree," Charlotte said promptly. "Better she should take her stutterer, who does seem a worthy young gentleman for all his nervousness. One could wish it would be appropriate to put a word in his ear to rush her off to Gretna Green. That would solve several difficulties."

"Charlotte!" Veronica stared at her sister.

Lady Elizabeth gave a crow of laughter. "You forget yourself, dear Charlotte. You are to hold down our flights of fancy!"

It was not surprising that Charlotte blushed. "I only said if it were appropriate, not that we should consider it for a moment."

"Still, we have hit upon the first consideration." Lady Elizabeth turned sober. "We must take each person involved in this muddle and decide how to direct them in the direction we would have them go."

"I am not at all pleased with Mr. Tonley as a prospective suitor for Rachel," Veronica said. "I have no wish to crowd our fences in that direction. The season has not even properly begun. There are so many eligible men for her to meet yet."

"Just so," Charlotte agreed. "The idea must be to draw Lord Beresford's attention from her. What would keep him busy?"

"A mill or a prizefight might do for a start," Veronica mused.

"No, drawing him off with sports will not do," Lady Elizabeth said and related the wager that led to his being in society. "I should have minded my own affairs."

"I've always been of the opinion that games of chance were not the best way to spend one's time," Charlotte said.

Veronica threw a sharp look at her sister, who was so deep in thought she did not see it. Nor did she see Lady Elizabeth's eyes flash with irritation. Charlotte was staring at the carpet in deep concentration, and spoke again without looking up.

"But what may be done with a deck of cards may be undone if chance falls right?" She turned a pair of pale, inquiring eyes on Lady Elizabeth.

"I see. A card party," Veronica said. "Lady Elizabeth—"

"Please call me Bess," Lady Elizabeth interrupted. "Conspirators should not stand on such ceremony."

"—Bess would lose this time and free Lord Beresford of his need to attend society parties, but would that gain us anything? Suppose he should choose to continue his pursuit of Rachel?"

"No, I do not think a game of cards would suffice as answer to our problem," Lady Elizabeth responded. "We are in need of rearranging the couples involved. I hope you do not mislike it, dear Veronica, but I have determined that you shall be my new sister."

Veronica's heart skipped, but she held her hopes in a firm grasp. "I should not wonder if your brother had other ideas."

"They must not signify," the widow retorted with the wisdom of one used to ordering the affairs of a loved one. "Who can trust a man to know what's good for him?"

"Charlotte's plight must also be taken into account," Veronica said slowly. "Had she not been so intent on extolling the supposed excellence of my mind, Lord Folkestone would have seen the superiority of hers."

At her sister's compliment Charlotte dropped her eyes; her modest smile softened her face to near beauty.

"We must also give some thought to a setting where she will be shown to be the woman he seeks," Veronica added.

Lady Elizabeth gave a cry of triumph. "Threebrookes Abbey! Nothing could be more perfect!"

When she saw the wondering expressions of her guests, she explained. "A ruin at Meadowreaches. It has been in the family for centuries, and was the bane of our lives. It was first an abbey, then a church, then—oh—I don't remember what else, but it comes complete with a history and an unpublished book of sermons that is the most fustian stuff imaginable—just right for Lord Folkestone...." Seeing the fire in Charlotte's eyes the widow paused in embarrassed confusion.

Veronica hurried to cover the faux pas. "Since he is always interested in delving into the philosophies of earlier times," she said.

"And you must know, Beresford can be thrown into the dumps by even thinking of it," Lady Elizabeth continued. "We were burdened with an uncle who spent his later years writing the history of it. He would read out long boring passages in the evenings. We lived in terror of the place." She laughed with delight. "You must convince Rachel that Julian would be most impressed if she could discuss the history with him."

"You have an evil mind," Veronica said, laughing. "I suddenly have the greatest desire to see this ruin."

They ceased their conversation perforce when the door opened and the butler and two footmen entered with a sumptuous tea. When the door closed again, Lady Elizabeth poured, giving little of her attention to the pot.

"We will make up a party, and I think I will also have a surprise for Beresford."

"Take care," Veronica warned as she took her cup. "He has a way of turning the tables on the plans of others."

"I am persuaded that Charlotte and you and I can prevent it if we keep our wits about us." Though they were seated a considerable distance from any door or window, she leaned forward, her voice low. "Now here is the way I think we should go about it...."

The three ladies spent a pleasant hour discussing just how they would arrange the party. Several times their murmured conversation was punctuated with laughter, but by the time the footmen came to remove the tea trays they were satisfied nothing could prevent them from succeeding.

When the Ivors' carriage was brought to the door to convey the young ladies back to Brook Street, Charlotte was clutching a leather-bound notebook containing the total writings of one Lord Frederick

Abbotsley, whose interest in the abbey had so nearly driven the young Abbotsleys to distraction.

The next morning the post brought an invitation from Lady Elizabeth to join a party of sightseers to visit the ruined Threebrookes Abbey. The trip was planned for three days hence, weather permitting.

"To walk around a collection of crumbling walls..." Lady Ellerbrook frowned at the delicate writing on the stiff folded paper.

"To absorb the history of a bygone age, Mama," Veronica corrected her gently. "I cannot find the past too interesting in books, but when one actually strolls the paths where the monks walked—"

"It does bring the past back so clearly," Charlotte added. "And one must not deprecate the invitation, because the Abbotsleys have owned the abbey for time out of mind."

"Abbey... Abbotsley..." Veronica let the implication trail off and hastily averted her eyes for fear Charlotte's raised eyebrows would cause her to laugh.

"One would not like to give offence..." Lady Ellerbrook murmured. "Thirty thousand pounds a year..."

"Lady Elizabeth was so kind as to lend me this history." Charlotte had brought the leather-bound notebook downstairs with her. "Both she and her brother are excessively proud of the place. They take it as a compliment when one knows something about it."

Lady Ellerbrook made no further complaint. Indeed, it was she who urged Rachel to peruse the book in order to speak intelligently to Lord Beresford on the subject. No one doubted he would be making one of

the party. His attentions to Rachel had kept Lady Ellerbrook in a flutter.

The morning of the scheduled venture dawned
bright and dry, with the promise of spring that had so
far eluded the weather. At a few minutes before eleven
o'clock, Squire Johns brought his phaeton to a halt in
front of Grimswell House. He was closely followed by
the rest of the party who had elected to ride. Lady
Elizabeth, Lords Beresford and Folkestone, Mr. Tonley and Major Lord Vermaine, a dashing officer in the
uniform of the Hungarian Hussars.

The major was the third son of the duke of Wen-
sley, a noble but impoverished house. Gossip did not
credit the major with being a fortune hunter precisely. He was tall and well-built with saturnine good
looks that must please. His address was polished and
his charm such that he kept feminine hearts aquiver.

While every hostess considered him an invaluable
asset to her guest list, hopeful mamas feared his influence on their susceptible daughters. It was said he
was indeed hanging out for a rich wife, but he knew
his own value and would settle for no less than the best
society could offer. Since this condemnation of his
character originated with parents of disappointed
damsels and rivals put out of the running by his presence, it was not much regarded.

Veronica had known Lady Elizabeth wanted to
spring an unwelcome surprise on her brother to pay
him back for the boorish company he had caused her
to endure. When she saw the major she smiled. The
earl would certainly have something to think about.

As the Westfield ladies descended the front steps and moved to the mounting block, it was clear Lord Beresford was not happy with the party, particularly with the inclusion of Mr. Tonley and the major.

"I wonder how Lady Elizabeth contrived to keep Beresford from including Lord Winsterfere or Mr. Oglethorpe," Charlotte murmured as she and Veronica followed Lady Ellerbrook and Rachel down the steps.

"I half suspected he would manage to miss this party," Veronica said. "It must be he did not know what was toward until too late."

When Lady Ellerbrook was seated in the squire's phaeton, that gentleman gave his horses the office to start, and they moved slowly down the street, clearing the way for the party of mounted riders to sort themselves out.

They were well aware that Beresford, if he were allowed to take command, would arrange matters his way. Determined that the earl would not be given a free hand, the ladies were ready to thwart him.

Charlotte must be partnered by the baron, and on the lengthy ride he would doubtless be brought to see the similarity of their sympathies. Mr. Tonley would escort Rachel and Lord Beresford, Veronica. The earl would also have the worry over the possibility of the major's charms affecting his sister and would have little time to think of Rachel.

Unfortunately for the conspirators, they had thrown the earl more of a facer than they knew. While he most certainly did not want his sister to fall prey to the charms of the major, he was equally ready to protect the Westfield ladies, and was thus in a quandary. As a result, he was hesitant, his usual decisiveness totally absent.

Veronica, Charlotte and Lady Elizabeth were counting heavily on the day bringing success to their plans. The tension they felt affected their mounts.

Sinbad, Charlotte's large and restive black, tossed his head and sidled to the left, causing Rachel to move quickly away or risk a collision. Her move put her next to Lord Folkestone. That gentleman, thinking she meant to ride at his side, urged his horse forward to partner her.

Since that pairing was no part of anyone's plan, both the earl and Charlotte turned in the direction of Rachel and the baron and found themselves riding together. Seeing their plans going astray, Lady Elizabeth jerked in the saddle as she turned wide eyes on Veronica. Taking the move to mean he was to fall in line, Lady Elizabeth's horse stepped forward. Clearly unhappy with events, Mr. Tonley set his mount forward at the same time. Veronica and the major brought up the rear of the cavalcade.

Veronica was torn between exasperation over the tangled plans and a desire to laugh, particularly when the procession rounded the corner. Both Charlotte and Beresford looked back on the other four riders. The earl's displeasure was evident. Charlotte's feelings were by that time under control, but her expression informed both Veronica and Lady Elizabeth that something had definitely gone amiss.

In her turn, Lady Elizabeth turned the corner, which gave her an opportunity to exchange glances with Veronica.

Her expression asked the question, "What happened?"

CHAPTER EIGHT

VERONICA BIT HER LIP to hide her smile and turned her attention to her escort. He at least was innocent of any machinations. Fairness demanded civility though she might be wishing him elsewhere.

"I do believe sir, that since we are the last of the column, we have the farthest to go." Her inane remark would at least serve to open a conversation.

"A pleasant day and charming company—I could not wish for a short ride," the major replied, his smile shining in his eyes.

Veronica had not been exposed to the major's charm before and its effect was striking. She was female enough to acknowledge its power. It even crossed her mind that, had her affections not been engaged, she might have felt a strong emotional response.

She could understand the earl's displeasure at having the major become an acquaintance of Lady Elizabeth. Veronica was equally determined to keep the major as far from Rachel and Charlotte as possible. He could never supersede the earl in any woman's affections, but she could not see the baron or Mr. Tonley holding a woman's heart against the fascinating major riding at her side.

Directly behind the phaeton, Rachel periodically nodded as Lord Folkestone talked, emphasizing his words with a shaking finger. Veronica wondered if a syllable had passed between Beresford and Charlotte, who rode so stiffly they could have been a set of matched figurines.

Lady Elizabeth was trying to draw out Mr. Tonley, and Veronica resigned herself to bear equally the hitch in their plans and attempt to rearrange matters after luncheon. She turned her attention to the major.

While it could not be said that she would have chosen his company, Veronica found the major an interesting companion. He had fought on the peninsula. Her questions elicited intelligent, articulate answers. Veronica spent an absorbing time assimilating the difference between managing a property and managing an army on the move. Almost two hours had passed before she gave a thought to the rest of the party.

When she next noticed the three mounted couples ahead, she was surprised. Lady Elizabeth had apparently found a subject in which Mr. Tonley's shyness was overridden by his interest. Judging by their alternate head shaking, Charlotte and Beresford were involved in some discussion in which they felt strong disagreement. Most surprising of all was the fact that the constantly prosing baron was nodding while Rachel held forth.

The party was then approaching the Grey Squirrel, a hostel known for its excellent food, where Lady Elizabeth had bespoken luncheon for the party.

Veronica was well satisfied to dismount but she looked about with determination. The plans of the morning had gone amiss, but she, Charlotte and Lady Elizabeth should certainly be able to rearrange the party to suit themselves.

She gave her left glove a resolute tug and watched as Charlotte jerked at the ribbons of her hat with equal determination. Charlotte's fleeting glance in her direction was a command to begin replanning immediately.

Unfortunately, Beresford also had ideas about ordering the party. He assisted Charlotte down from her horse, and led her back to stand with Lady Elizabeth and Mr. Tonley. With a haughty look at his sister, he continued past them and walked up to where Veronica and Major Lord Vermaine were standing.

"Vermaine, I don't think you've had the pleasure of being presented to Lady Ellerbrook," he said casually. "I'll do the honours for you."

"Delighted," the major replied, his brows slightly raised, but the invitation had been so bluntly put, he could only acquiesce.

Veronica knew the earl too well to believe his offer augured well for their plans. She stiffened her intention in the face of the direct move by the earl, but he forestalled her. As they caught up with Lady Elizabeth, Mr. Tonley and Charlotte, Beresford gave Veronica a smile that portended more than friendliness.

"Do you know the history of the Grey Squirrel, Miss Westfield?"

Veronica recognized the opening of a tactical manoeuvre, though she wasn't sure what it was to accomplish. She would not let him get away with his plan.

"Of course," she answered with composure.

The earl blinked and she congratulated herself on throwing him off balance. Unfortunately he was quick to recover.

"Then do tell my sister, she is most interested in hearing it." Taking the major's arm, the earl led the soldier toward Lady Ellerbrook and the squire.

Lady Elizabeth and Veronica exchanged glances, but Charlotte was watching as Lord Folkestone and Rachel approached the door of the inn, walking slowly, totally engrossed in their conversation.

"Shall we try to catch up to my sister and the baron?" she asked brightly. "I confess I'm agog to hear their interesting conversation."

"Mmm...most certainly." Mr. Tonley hurried along at Charlotte's side, leaving Lady Elizabeth and Veronica to bring up the rear of the party. As the two young ladies strolled together, Lady Elizabeth glanced up at Veronica.

"I hope you will not take it amiss if I say you are not my notion of the perfect escort."

Veronica gave a quick shake of her head. "There are far too many cooks stirring this pudding."

"And my odious brother is adding a flavour I do not care for. Perhaps I do you a disservice in trying to save him from Rachel."

Veronica smiled. "I fear we had better save Rachel from Charlotte."

As they approached the door, they saw Rachel and the baron enter. The earl was busy ordering the party so the major followed, then Lady Ellerbrook and Beresford. Charlotte and Mr. Tonley had not been in time to overtake the first couple and they entered behind the squire.

When Veronica and the young widow had traversed the dim flagstone passage and stepped into the large private parlour, they stopped and exchanged outraged looks.

The room was not fitted with one large table as Lady Elizabeth had supposed, but with four smaller ones. Lord Folkestone and Rachel had been shown to a table with only two chairs. The earl had somehow managed to get the major and Lady Ellerbrook to a larger table, but had placed his whip and hat in the fourth chair.

Unable to join that set, the squire had stepped over to the other large table, reluctantly accompanied by Charlotte and Mr. Tonley.

"Beyond permission," Lady Elizabeth hissed as she led the way to the unoccupied table, set apart from the others. The young widow dropped in a chair with a pout as she voiced her frustrations.

"It occurs to me that there is a large, abandoned well at Threebrookes Abbey, and since it has a reputation for being haunted, none of the Meadowreaches people will go near it."

"But how do we push Beresford in it?" Veronica asked, perfectly understanding the situation.

"We'll enlist Charlotte's aid." Suddenly Lady Elizabeth's eyes began to twinkle. "No, she'd want to send

Rachel with him, which is what we particularly wish to avoid." Her bottom lip protruded slightly as she cast a dissatisfied glance in the direction of her brother. "I confess I don't understand his latest start."

"Who," Veronica asked, her own eyes taking on a glimmer of humour, "is the one female in the party not likely to become enamoured of the major?"

"Oh, may I be granted patience," Lady Elizabeth muttered. "He is protecting all of us—I see. Perhaps I was a little too forward in my choice of companions, but I did want to give him a setback after Oglethorpe and Winsterfere."

"You certainly threw the cat among the pigeons," Veronica said.

For the moment their conversation came to a halt as they were served with an excellent game pie, thinly sliced roast venison and fresh asparagus.

Once they had given lip service to the more violent of their emotions, they formulated another plan over strawberry tarts.

"Your brother will doubtless try to arrange things himself," Veronica warned Lady Elizabeth as they pulled on their gloves and led the way down the dim corridor to the inn yard.

"Let him." The little widow smiled thoughtfully. "The distance is short. We'll soon be there, and our acquiescence now will lull him into thinking he's won."

But though the earl thought himself well able to order the party, he reckoned without the other gentlemen present. Major Lord Vervaine handed Lady Ellerbrook into the phaeton and then strode over to

Veronica, saying he would be pleased to throw her into the saddle, and they could continue their discussion.

Veronica gave Lady Elizabeth a quick look and wondered how she could gently refuse, but the viscountess had her own problems. Mr. Tonley might lack the ease of conversation expected in a gentleman with town bronze, but he had a keen sense of duty. He led the widow's horse over, preparing to help her into the saddle.

Since Rachel and the baron were still talking easily, the earl was left to escort Charlotte.

Veronica was glad when the party turned from the road and rode up a lane. A short way from the road, hidden behind a knoll, were the ruins of Threebrookes Abbey.

Despite her displeasure over the thwarted plans and her indifference to history, Veronica was enchanted.

The maze of roofless stone walls rose to varying heights, none more than ten feet, and created doorless alcoves with smooth grass floors. Many of the walls reached no more than two or three feet high and created walks where ancient passages, long destroyed, had once been.

Through the years, seedlings had grown to saplings and into mature trees in the areas where monks had worked and slept and worshipped. In the shade, moss and lichen had taken hold. The stone walls were varicoloured with age and dappled with deep shade.

Disturbed by the visitors, a small herd of goats leapt over the low walls at the other end of the ruin; their presence showed why the thick lush grass seemed so well trimmed.

"Methinks our hostess made a grave error in her plans," the major said softly as they viewed the ruins from horseback.

"You don't care for it?" Veronica was surprised.

"*Au contraire*, I like it well enough to think a picnic luncheon would have been more the thing." He pointed to an area where several turnings in the stone walls were overhung by the limbs of a huge oak and the play of sun and shadow produced a sylvan quality. "I confess a desire to explore that section."

"Perhaps an ancient monk will appear and regale you with the history of the abbey." Veronica laughed.

"From the scraps of conversation I've heard, I think I do not need a monk," the major said. "Pray protect me from a lecture from one of your well-educated sisters."

Veronica smiled, and hoped the manners she was trying to assume looked more genuine than they felt. It was no part of her plan to spend her time with the major.

Rachel and Lord Folkestone had dismounted and left their horses with the groom who had ridden ahead to be of service. After calling a gay word to her mother, Rachel walked off on the arm of Lord Folkestone before the other ladies had dismounted.

Veronica was shocked and displeased, and not much reassured when she noticed the couple had not actually entered the ruins but had stopped once they were out of earshot of the rest. They had signified, by their continued conversation, that they were finding pleasure in each other's company, and nothing short of a blatant effort would split them apart.

Veronica watched with dissatisfaction as Beresford and Charlotte, for once in agreement, started purposefully toward the couple. By their faces, they were determined either to separate Folkestone and Rachel, or to provide the censorious atmosphere of disapproving chaperons.

By that time the rest of the party had dismounted, and after a despairing look at Veronica, Lady Elizabeth took Mr. Tonley's arm and hurried him toward the other two couples.

"Miss Charlotte," she called, the forced gaiety in her voice sounding a little shrill. "You might be interested in starting your exploration in the nave of the church. I believe the visit will offer more if you begin there."

Charlotte perforce had to stop and turn toward Lady Elizabeth. The harried look in her eye was obvious as she tried to find some recourse to avoid turning back from her pursuit of Rachel and the baron.

"Of course, you're right." Not prone to dissimulation, Charlotte sounded even more artificial than Lady Elizabeth. "Just a moment, and we will bring back Rachel and Lord Folkestone. They will also wish to begin at the beginning."

Rachel and the baron had walked on, their pace giving no evidence they wished to escape from the party, but their path had taken them around a wall and out of sight. Charlotte caught the earl's arm, and only his sure footedness kept him from being jerked forward.

"I think we should forgo that interesting nook for the moment and also head for the nave," the major murmured.

"Oh?" Veronica looked up at him. "I thought you eschewed history when possible."

"I do, but I confess a keen desire to know what goes forward." He gave her a knowing smile. "I'm coming to realize I, too, have a part in this farce, but I have not yet been able to discover what it is."

"The party was not of my making," Veronica replied, not willing to tell him he had been invited to discomfit the earl of Beresford.

Charlotte and Beresford had disappeared around the stone wall that hid Rachel and the baron from the sight of the rest of the party. As the other three couples waited, they heard a sudden sharp cry—a woman in pain.

"Rachel! Charlotte!" Lady Ellerbrook, who was standing behind Veronica, cried out and brushed past her eldest daughter.

Veronica allowed the squire to pass as he hurried to offer the plump little woman help. She followed behind Lady Elizabeth and Mr. Tonley, who were nearly treading on the heels of the older couple.

As they rounded the wall, they were in time to see the earl carrying Charlotte to a seat on a low section of stone. Rachel was following closely, holding out a vinaigrette. The baron was hovering just at the edge of the action. Beresford looked up at the approach of the others.

"Take care," he called out sharply. "That grass hides some treacherous places."

Veronica was to discover he was right as she and the major brought up the end of the party. The goats had grazed the grass smooth, but beneath the camouflaging growth fallen stones made the walkway uneven.

Though Lady Ellerbrook was not brilliant, and seldom kept a thought in her head long enough to complete it, she was a mother who could be counted upon when one of her brood was in trouble. She turned on the gentlemen and ordered them back around the turn of the path. When they had disappeared, she knelt to inspect Charlotte's ankle.

"Mama, I've done no more than turn it," Charlotte said, her voice sharp. "I cannot believe I have been so stupid."

"Are you sure?" Rachel knelt by her mother, all concern.

In answer, Charlotte put her foot on the ground, tried to put some weight on it and winced before raising it again.

"I have most definitely turned it," she said.

Lady Ellerbrook whimpered in sympathy.

"I'd be in far more pain if it were broken," Charlotte said bracingly. She turned apologetically toward Lady Elizabeth. "I must apologize for being such a ninny."

"I must take Charlotte back to town," Lady Ellerbrook announced suddenly. "I am sorry to ruin your party..." she said to Lady Elizabeth, letting her words trail off. It was not to be supposed that she could continue such decisiveness for very long.

"We must all take Charlotte back to town," Lady Elizabeth said. "I will be glad to have this fiasco behind us."

Lady Ellerbrook and Rachel looked with wonder on the solemn understanding nods that passed between Lady Elizabeth, Veronica and Charlotte. They had no time to ask, because Lady Elizabeth called to the earl and the gentlemen came back to join the party.

Lord Beresford carried Charlotte to the phaeton. It did not need to be said that the others would ride back immediately behind the vehicle.

When they mounted their horses, it was Mr. Tonley who stepped forward to give assistance to Lady Ellerbrook, who was in some distress. He tenderly assisted her to mount Sinbad, Charlotte's horse, and ranged himself by her side.

To Lady Elizabeth's astonishment and chagrin, the baron was moved to range on her side as her major defender, assuring her no blame could attach itself to her. Moreover, he told her she had indeed provided a spiritually elevating excursion, even if it had been cut short. He helped her to mount, and announced he would be her support on the return journey.

Standing by the phaeton, Veronica could hardly contain her mirth when she glimpsed the young widow's face. But she was not so pleased when the major gave his support to Rachel. Even knowing that this pairing of the couples for the return journey meant she would be in the earl's company was insufficient to ward off a feeling of dread at seeing her beautiful sister in close proximity to the major's charm.

Lady Ellerbrook and Mr. Tonley rode directly behind the phaeton. Rachel and the major fell in after them, with Lady Elizabeth and the baron next in line.

"Poor Charlotte," Beresford commented to Veronica when they had left the lane and were on the public road again. "I hope her accident will not keep her housebound for long."

"I doubt it will," Veronica replied. "She seems to think a little rest will cure it. Mama will insist a physician sees it."

"Lady Ellerbrook is sensible," Beresford said. "Charlotte's courage should not be allowed to overrun good sense."

"Charlotte?" Veronica laughed, but seeing his startled expression she quickly sobered. "I must seem heartless to you, but I know her too well. She will make no more of her injury than is justified, and not a whit less. Her dislike of illness is so strong she will not risk prolonging it by overusing that ankle."

"A most intelligent attitude—and after this morning I should not be surprised by it."

Even in his praise, Veronica could hear in his voice the boredom he had suffered. She was neither surprised nor insulted, but amused that her sister's most admirable qualities could so weary the earl. He noticed her amusement.

"How did you manage it?" he asked softly, a dangerous gleam in his eye. "I confess, I have not yet seen your strategy, and for my own safety I had better discover it."

Veronica could not keep back her laugh. "Put your fears to rest, I had no hand in arranging the party."

"I beg leave not to believe you. Not even Bess could have so crossed me."

"I did not do it," Veronica answered him in irritation. "If the hand had been mine, would I be allowing Rachel to come under the influence of the handsome major?"

"No, I don't think you would," the earl agreed, looking up the column of riders.

"It's also unfortunate that Rachel and the baron are getting along so well. That was no one's intention."

"Perhaps I should retire from the lists," the earl said amiably. "I have no desire to emulate a stutterer or to prose on about various churchmen through the ages."

Veronica kept her eyes on the road and said nothing. She had allowed Lady Elizabeth's enthusiasm to give her hope, but now, riding beside the earl in the full awareness of her feelings for him, she was overwhelmed by his presence. The subtlety of his sensual nature invaded her senses like a fine cologne. She was intensely aware of his poise and good looks.

She had never considered herself even passable in beauty and found it impossible to believe he would ever see her as anything more than a chance companion whose wit had lightened a few moments of his life.

"I admit to being in a quandary," he said slowly. "My sister ordered the party. Squire Johns was definitely invited to escort your mother, Tonley for Rachel, and Folkestone for Charlotte. Was the major invited to entertain you or to irritate me by being her escort?"

The earl's reading of the arrangements was masterly, but as he neared the end of his assumptions he was placing both himself and Veronica in a delicate position. His pause warned her of the direction of his thoughts, and she felt the colour rise in her cheeks. She turned her head away.

"And the major worries me," Beresford went on hurriedly. "Now it seems he has turned his charms on Rachel."

"No, I don't like that, either," Veronica said, looking up the line of riders. Rachel was fast loosing her shyness. That morning she had been in easy converse with the baron, and now she was laughing with the major.

But Veronica had her own problems. The earl had not forgotten where his ruminations had led him. He was riding with less poise; his attention was too strictly trained on the road ahead.

Veronica's heart sank. She was sure he had realized the attempt to manipulate him, and he disliked it.

At least one concrete fact had come from the outing. She must give up all hope of winning the earl's love.

CHAPTER NINE

A FEW DAYS after the ill-fated trip to Threebrookes Abbey, Amabelle was also to take part in an outing equally displeasing to her.

On a certain sunny afternoon she sat beneath a tree in Richmond Park, heartily wishing she had listened to her older sisters.

As Veronica had prophesied, Amabelle had indeed overcome her mother's restrictions. She had half convinced Lady Ellerbrook any gossip about the Brentwoods was put about by hopeful mamas whose daughters couldn't compare in looks to Elsa and the twins. Judicious reminders of the proposed school at Red Oaks had stiffened her mother's back against the accusations of her two oldest daughters. Still, Amabelle had found it difficult to override her mother's doubts. Tears and pleas had not overcome Lady Ellerbrook's decree, but Amabelle's solemn promise to avoid any exceptionable behaviour and circumstances had sufficed.

Amabelle had intended to keep her promise, and was uncomfortably aware her recent behaviour had been abominable.

Hers were acts born of desperation. She had long known her dear but flighty mother was ruled in practical matters by the superior intelligence of Veronica and Charlotte, and while they consented to this one season, they might never again set foot within the exalted circles of London society. Amabelle herself was practical enough to know that if her sisters were adamant in remaining in the country, her mother would not leave them alone at Red Oaks in order to bring Amabelle back to London next year.

Before the family had been in London a week, she knew she had been in error in leaving Miss Filibrew's Seminary for Young Ladies. She was without the company of her school friends, and her mama and sisters were taken up with the exigencies of the season. With neither her studies nor social activities to fill her time, Amabelle had tended to brood and build a sense of injustice, as she wallowed in the misfortune of being a year too young for her come-out.

In her fear and disappointment, tears always seemed to be gathering behind Amabelle's lids. She longed for a happier time when she could have taken all her problems to Veronica. Even Charlotte, for all her prudishness, had occasionally helped Amabelle to hide some innocent little escapade, after a scold, of course.

But Amabelle was aware she had alienated her sisters, with full justification on their part. Nor could she fault them for their censure of her actions on Bond Street. She had honourably stood by Nora and Nolly, but in truth, the twins had accidentally come upon two guardsmen and abandoned her. Amabelle had been aware she could be the object of gossip. Her sense of ill-use had doubled.

She had fought valiantly to defend herself and the Brentwoods, but she knew if she were drawn too deeply into their escapades her family would suffer. Before she had given her mother her word to behave with more circumspection, she had laid that same stricture on herself.

But even in her young eyes her promise was now broken. After the incident on Bond Street, Amabelle had made it plain to the young Brentwood ladies that she was not in favour of secret meetings with soldiers. Their apologies had been prolific and had sounded truly sincere. Nor would Amabelle have sought permission to attend the picnic, if the plans had not included Lady Brentwood, whose presence made it unexceptional.

The young ladies had chosen to ride to Richmond Park accompanied by a groom. Amabelle had not been told they were to be joined by several young officers from the Life Guards.

Lady Brentwood was to travel by carriage. But when a Brentwood vehicle arrived at the designated picnic area, it held only a maid, a footman and an elaborate picnic lunch. An inquiry for her hostess elicited a casual reply from Elsa Brentwood that her mother had considered the day much too cool and had elected to attend an engagement in town.

Amabelle was shocked at the impropriety of the situation but she was also nonplussed. Her own sense of correctness was offended, and she could just imagine what Charlotte would say.

But what could she do? She did not dare return to town unescorted, nor did she wish to offend the

Brentwoods sufficiently to break the connection entirely. They were her only friends in town; she had not cultivated any others.

It occurred to her that she would save embarrassment and be returned home most speedily with a proper chaperon if she were ill. But when she pleaded a severe headache, Elsa Brentwood recommended, with scarcely veiled irritation, that she sit quietly under a tree and not ruin the excursion for the others.

Not knowing what else to do, Amabelle remained at the picnic site seeking what little social protection was afforded by the Brentwood servants. The three Brentwood sisters, all in high gig, strolled around the banks of the pond at the foot of the hill and fed the ducks with bread left over from the repast.

As Amabelle watched, the occasional discomfort she had previously explained away reared itself too abruptly to be ignored. She was finally facing the fact that the Brentwoods were not, in the terms of society, quite the thing. Nora and Nolly were cavorting about laughing at their escorts, as the lieutenants Morington and Vincent attempted to call the ducks by quacking. And Amabelle could not think the way Miss Elsa Brentwood clung to the arm of Captain Lawrence proper behaviour.

But if the Brentwood ladies had seen fit to desert their guest, they had not left Amabelle totally bereft of company, an imposition that made her feel even more put upon.

A few days before, she had thought Lieutenant Cartwright's saturnine good looks, the slightly ironic curve of his lips and his tall elegant frame made him the most fascinating man in London. Indeed, his visits to Brentwood House had played a large part in her determination to remain friends with Nora and Nolly.

She had taken the twins into her breathless confidence concerning her new love, and had been much astounded when Nolly, the more practical of the two, had taken Amabelle's affair of the heart as something to be speedily handled.

"You must know he is rolled up and a dowry of twenty thousand pounds would interest him exceedingly," the youngest of the Misses Brentwood told her friend.

Amabelle was much embarrassed when the gentleman immediately began to show a marked interest in her.

With the ambiguous fantasies of a young lady not truly out of the schoolroom, Amabelle would have been content to admire the dashing officer from afar. She would have sighed over his every glance in her general direction, read in his most casual words a double meaning and suffered the delicious pangs of unrequited love.

She was addicted to penny novels when she could hide them from the family and her teachers at school; she knew true love was beset with heartbreaking obstacles to be borne with heroic fortitude, betrayed only by trembling lips and eyes bright with tears.

To have the object of her affection literally at her feet—for Lieutenant Cartwright was sitting on a rug directly in front of her—was contrary to her ideas of romance in the highest sense. It infected her with a strong sense of discomfort. She was unpleasantly aware of his scrutiny as she sat considering the difficulty of her situation.

To prevent a tête-à-tête, she had kept her eyes closed as she leaned back against an obliging tree. Occasionally she peeked beneath her lowered lashes when her distress and restlessness would not allow her mind to be still. The others in the party were returning from the lake.

"Smith, is there any lemonade left?" Nolly called to the footman who was preparing to load a stone crock into the carriage.

Amabelle opened her eyes and shifted. Surely, had she been thought to be asleep, the activity would have awakened her.

"Shall I get you a glass?" Lieutenant Cartwright asked her, rising from his position on the rug as the ladies approached.

"Thank you, no." Amabelle attempted to sound weak and listless as the three Brentwood ladies approached. "I declare I am most sincerely ashamed of having dampened the spirits of the party by being out of sorts," she said to Elsa, "but I think I have hit on a solution."

"You feel much more the thing," Elsa said bracingly.

"Indeed I do not," Amabelle denied. "But if you have no objection, I will return in the carriage with the servants." She was dismayed when, instead of immediately agreeing, Miss Elsa Brentwood seemed irritated.

"If you feel you must, there is no help for it," she said. "But I am persuaded my mother would feel it incumbent upon us to return with you, so the party is ruined in any case."

Amabelle had railed at her sisters because they did not see her point of view, but she had never before been faced with a selfishness that ignored the discomfort of others. She was some moments attempting to find a way of countering Elsa's unfeeling remark.

"You must feel better by now," Nora said, adding her view to her sister's. "And we have planned such a lovely ride back to Brook Street. I cannot think the carriage would get you there any faster. It's a battered old thing and too out-of-date to be seen in."

"I think you had better ride with us." Miss Brentwood gave her ruling, which Amabelle could not gainsay without the necessity of a disagreeable scene.

"If you are returning directly to Brook Street, I daresay you are right," Amabelle said slowly. Her concern really had produced the headache to which she had laid claim. She would be more comfortable riding on Corsair, her smooth-gaited bay gelding than in the carriage, which did indeed look old and ill-sprung.

While they had been discussing the situation, the groom had brought up the riding animals, and Amabelle allowed Lieutenant Cartwright to throw her into the saddle. She was relieved that the others mounted with little ado. But when Elsa and Captain Lawrence led off the mounted expedition she noticed they were headed in the opposite direction from which they had arrived.

"Should we not be going the other way?" Amabelle asked anxiously.

Elsa Brentwood threw her a look of impatient dislike. "If you are wishful to return to Brook Street immediately, I should think you would be glad of the shortest path." Elsa led the way forward with a toss of her head.

The youngest Miss Westfield was not much reassured, though she could do little but follow the rest of the party. Each partnered by an escort, the twins had immediately followed Miss Brentwood. Amabelle and Lieutenant Cartwright were left to bring up the rear of the expedition.

They rode some distance on a track wide enough to travel side by side. When they turned on a narrow track through a copse, Lieutenant Cartwright pulled his horse in just ahead of Corsair and gradually slowed the pace until the others were out of sight.

"Perhaps we should hasten along," Amabelle said, acutely aware of being alone with the officer.

But instead of taking her suggestion and speeding his animal, he slowed and turned it across the path blocking her way. "I think you need a rest," he said. "We are moving too speedily for your comfort."

Drawing Corsair to an abrupt halt, Amabelle could feel herself pale under his scrutiny and despised her fears, knowing her reaction was giving support to his remark.

"I want to go home," she countered, feeling the tears gather.

"I almost feel it is my company you wish to eschew," he answered, taking upon himself a slightly injured air.

"Oh, no!" Amabelle was not willing to admit the truth outright.

She had at first considered him dashing in the extreme, but she wondered why she had ever thought the ironic turn to the corner of his mouth attractive. In her present mood, she took that facial expression as a clear sign of cruelty. She allowed it to feed the fears that had been building in her since she had first discovered Lady Brentwood was not chaperoning the party.

Lieutenant Cartwright took her hesitation as acquiescence and reached out to catch her hand.

"You must know, my dear one," he said, looking deeply into her frightened eyes, "that I have, from the moment of first seeing you, been overwhelmed by your beauty."

Amabelle attempted to draw her hand away, but Lieutenant Cartwright was far more experienced in the ways of young ladies than Amabelle could have imagined. He clasped it ever more tightly and raised it to his lips.

Panicked by his overtures, Amabelle released all pressure on the reins and with her right leg sharply slapped Corsair's shoulder.

From long understanding of the command, the bay gelding reared, flailing his hoofs.

"Wha-a-a?" In attempting to dodge the bay's iron-shod forefeet, Lieutenant Cartwright drew his horse sharply back. Amabelle took advantage of her freedom, wheeled Corsair round and raced in the direction from which they came, travelling at full gallop.

Behind her, she could hear the pounding of the lieutenant's horse as he shouted her name and demanded she halt, his voice carrying all the accents of the cruelty she had read in his mouth.

Amabelle had little fear of being overtaken. The finest rider in London would have been privileged to throw a leg over Corsair's back, and it was well-known in the region of Red Oaks that the Westfield ladies could "outride the devil himself."

By the time she had reached the end of the narrow track and had turned back on the wider path of the park, Amabelle had formed a plan. She was confident the Brentwood carriage would have returned in the direction from which they had approached Richmond Park. Even if it had by that time left the picnic site, she would easily overtake it. Nor was she long in coming upon the area in which they had partaken of their luncheon. She was still not much concerned about her ability to overtake the carriage when she discovered the servants had already left for their return trip to Brook Street.

But only moments later she realized the error in her plan. Since the party had arrived in Richmond Park by horseback, they had not been constrained to remain on the carriage paths. She saw, leading off to the side, the smaller, rougher track they had used to approach the picnic area. Logic suggested that if she continued in the direction the carriage must have gone, she would overtake it. But a second check to her plans soon appeared in the shape of a fork in the road. She slackened Corsair's pace while she attempted to reason out which way the Brentwood carriage had travelled.

Accustomed to riding the countryside around Red Oaks, Amabelle had a well-developed sense of direction. Unfortunately, the road curved and both branches of the fork appeared equally likely to return her to Mayfair and Brook Street. While she was considering, the whinny of a horse somewhere behind convinced her Lieutenant Cartwright must be on her trail. She fled down the right fork.

She was a light burden on the back of her magnificent mount and, not restrained by citified manners, he carried her at a spanking pace for another score of minutes before she considered the effect on passersby of a lone young lady at full gallop.

She slowed her pace and had continued another half hour before it occurred to her that she had not once had need to duck her head to dodge some inquiring matron's disapproving gaze. The lack of that necessity brought on a fresh fear. At this season Richmond Park was a popular area for the ton. If she'd seen no evidence of the social set then her choice at the fork had not been the correct one.

What should she do? Should she return to the fork in the park? To do so would mean a full hour's delay in reaching home. She knew it was far past teatime. She might encounter Lieutenant Cartwright or the Brentwoods.

Travelling back to Brook Street in the company of the entire party was much preferable to riding alone, but Amabelle was in lively fear lest she once again be left in the company of the fortune-hunting officer, as she now termed him. And if she did not find the party she could be lost again.

No, she thought, pausing to think over the situation. She had taken the right fork when she should have turned to the left. Therefore, to the left and somewhere ahead lay Mayfair and Brook Street.

She was in an unsavoury area, journeying along littered streets and being watched by hard-eyed city dwellers. Then a possible solution to her dilemma approached in the person of a jarvey perched upon the high seat of a public hack.

She hailed the driver, who eyed her with rude speculation. Her circumstances and the expression on the man's face caused her voice to tremble slightly as she asked directions to Brook Street.

The driver eyed her narrowly and rubbed the stubble on his chin thoughtfully.

"Aye, I reckon I could get there," he said slowly, "but working out the directions in my head will take some thought, it will." Removing his grimy hand from his chin, he held it out in her direction cupped, as if to receive some payment in return for the effort he was about to make.

Amabelle would have been delighted to pay for the information had she been able to do so.

"I-I have no money about me," she said, "but if you will give me the direction and your name, I would be happy to leave your payment with my footman for a time when you chanced to be in Brook Street and could collect."

"Aye, and I'm going to come all that way for one copper penny. Once my lady has what she seeks, the value will be gone, it will," the jarvey said, his eyes filled with avarice and discontent as he stared at Amabelle, his gaze focusing on the gold locket around her neck and then moving to take in Corsair's blood lines. "But how would it be, my lady, if you was to tie that handsome creature to the back of me hack and I was to deliver you to Brook Street?"

Amabelle was ready to accept the suggestion, when she saw the jarvey direct a speaking look to two loiterers standing outside a disreputable inn. Having been an avid reader of the most time-wasting literature, Amabelle was struck with a sudden vision of being taken to some dark den where her locket and Corsair would be taken from her, and she would probably be held for ransom.

"Thank you, no," she said suddenly and whipped Corsair into a gallop, which she continued until she felt a safe distance from the jarvey and his friends.

Not daring to approach anyone else, she wound back and forth among strange streets. Twilight was deepening when the houses on her way became large and more respectable.

Corsair had picked up a stone and was favouring his right foreleg. Amabelle was dizzy with a pounding in her head and a most excruciating thirst when she came abreast of a couple walking along a street.

The young man was in the livery of a footman, and accompanying him was a young woman in the plain cloak worn by maids in respectable households. They were obviously interested in each other and did not look up until Amabelle brought her mount to a halt and asked for directions.

Amabelle was reassured by their help, but she flinched at the shock and curiosity in their eyes. She hurried on as fast as Corsair's limp would allow. She had long before resigned herself to the fact that she

would face the strictest censure from Charlotte.
Veronica was often far more understanding; however, her disapproval of Amabelle's latest escapade
would be implacable. But Amabelle would almost
welcome their disapproving remarks; it would mean
she was safely back in Brook Street again.

Her fears were ebbing and she was just deciding she
had come through a harrowing experience relatively
unscathed, when she turned onto Mount Street.

She was almost in sight of Spinford House when a
party of gentlemen appeared around the corner from
Brook Street. They were clearly in their cups, holding
hands to form a chain across the way as they sang a
popular drinking song. In justice to the revellers, they
had not intended to block her path and were as surprised to discover a young woman alone on horseback as Amabelle was dismayed to have met them.

Her startled movement brought Corsair to a halt,
and for a few seconds the one young lady and the six
merrymakers stared at one another in equal amaze-
ment.

The tall, elegantly dressed gentleman at the left end
of the chain released his friend's arm and, doffing his
hat, gave Amabelle a deep bow. "Your servant, my
lady," he said in the slurred accents of one who most
assuredly had imbibed too much. Then looking down
the line of gentlemen with a bleary eye, he called out,
"I say, you ill-bred farmers, break the chain and allow the lady to pass."

One of those holding the middle of the street was a
pinch-faced, ill-featured young man who took exception to the gallant gentleman's remark. He clasped his

friends' hands even tighter. "The Haymarket is in the other direction," he twittered, giggling at what he meant as a humorous remark.

He had overstepped himself and shocked his companions. Two of the gentlemen immediately hustled out of Amabelle's path.

Her cheeks flaming, Amabelle rode on without a word, fervently hoping she had not been recognized. But the strident voice coming behind her verified her every fear.

"I don't know why you're so upset," the ill-mannered gentleman was expostulating to his friends. "It's only that Westfield chit. She keeps company with the Brentwoods, so judge for yourself what she is."

CHAPTER TEN

WHILE AMABELLE WAS SUFFERING her painful lesson, Veronica and Rachel took luncheon at Lady Markham's. Later they made an excursion to Bond Street where they purchased a new bonnet for Veronica and a book for Charlotte, who was curtailing her walking giving her wrenched ankle time to heal completely.

Charlotte had proved as sensible about her injury as Veronica had prophesied. After resting it for a day, she had resumed a modified schedule of social activities, eschewing shopping excursions, dancing and their customary afternoon strolls in Hyde Park.

Veronica and Rachel returned home to discover that Lady Elizabeth had called while they were out. She had scribbled a message to Veronica and left it in a twist.

Tomorrow I Must return home Temporarily. Will Attempt to see you for some Private Conversation before leaving. If Not, do Nothing before my Return.

The Westfields were engaged to attend the theatre that evening in company with Lord Beresford and

Lady Elizabeth, but there would be no opportunity for any "private conversation" between the two ladies.

"The only person in the world on my side and she must needs leave London," Veronica moaned as she showed the note to Charlotte.

"I beg your pardon?" Charlotte stiffened in affront. "I'm Bonaparte, I suppose?"

"Oh, forgive me, dear Charlotte, but I so count on you that you're like a part of me."

This compliment soothed Charlotte's ruffled feelings, and the sisters parted above stairs, each retiring to her own room to contemplate her difficulties. They did not meet again until teatime, when they gathered with Lady Ellerbrook and Rachel in the back drawing room.

At Charlotte's inquiry, Lady Ellerbrook announced Amabelle had a previous engagement. Charlotte was unable to follow up this remark because her mother quickly changed the subject. Veronica had, upon her return from her walk, sought out her youngest sister and knew Amabelle had been allowed to accompany the Misses Brentwood to Richmond Park. But her own problems had overridden her concern about Amabelle's waywardness and her mother's lack of firmness in handling her.

Veronica watched her mother as she suddenly became locquacious in discussing the ball of the previous night. She spoke almost exclusively with Rachel. Charlotte seemed taken up with her own thoughts for a time. Then with a conspiratorial glance toward Veronica, she addressed Rachel.

"My dear, I cannot think how it is that last night's affair became such a tangle. I for one do apologize most humbly for not spending more time in your company."

The rest of the family turned startled glances on Charlotte. Though she might be most diligent in her duty to the family, she had not previously considered the chaperonage of Rachel any part of her responsibility.

Since the remark was addressed to her, Rachel gazed at her sister with no little confusion. "I cannot think what you mean." Then pausing, she looked up, her eyes widening, filled with dread. "Can it be that I overstepped propriety?"

"Pooh, most assuredly not! I doubt you are capable of doing so," Veronica said in defence of Rachel's behaviour. She was curious about Charlotte's intentions.

"No, I was speaking of your being so much in the company of the earl of Beresford," Charlotte said. "I remember your remark the other day—you said that gentleman throws you into a quake. I cannot think it well done of us—" She was interrupted by a trill of laughter from Rachel.

"Nor can I think how I could have been so goosish," Rachel said. "Julian—the earl—is the most charming of gentlemen—" with this she threw a bright gaze in Veronica's direction before turning back to Charlotte "—and he is by no means the ogre I feared he would be."

"Well he is showing you the most marked attention," Charlotte said crisply. "And I do wish you would take a care for the time you spend in his company. Surely he is not a gentleman for whom you could develop a tendre—"

"How not?" Rachel interrupted in surprise. "I am persuaded his wealth and position—along with his other attributes—must make him by far the most attractive catch in London."

"Catch!" Veronica ejaculated, finding even her own sensibilities much shaken by that phrase. She had not missed Rachel's hastily covered use of Beresford's name.

"Oh, quite," Rachel said, rising to replace her cup on the tea tray. "And since we are to accompany him and Lady Elizabeth to the theatre tonight, if you will excuse me, I am not much satisfied with the dress I had chosen to wear...." And with that she tripped hastily from the room, leaving her mother and her sisters staring at one another in dismay.

"I do not believe what I heard," Charlotte announced when the door was closed. "I am persuaded that—that—attitude could not have come from Rachel. Speaking of wealth and position in that way! She's always been as heedless as Amabelle about such things."

Lady Ellerbrook would have protested at the remark, but she was not allowed the chance. Veronica also rose and went hurriedly to her room, her feelings much abraded by hearing the man she most admired relegated to a commodity on the marketplace.

At first her head had told her Rachel and Lord Beresford must each find within the other personable qualities not to be ignored. But then, as her feelings for the earl had grown, her heart had defied logic and assured her they were indifferent to each other. Unable to give way to the pain welling up inside her, she let her mind go blank, sinking into dumb misery. She wasn't aware of the passing of time. Later, after lightly tapping on the door, Charlotte softly opened it and entered, closing it behind her.

"You haven't begun to dress," she said, and Veronica realized her sister was already prepared for the evening's excursion to the theatre.

"I suppose I must go," Veronica said listlessly, rising and reaching for the bellpull to call her dresser.

But Charlotte waved her away from it. "I'll assist you," she said, "and mayhap we can think of an answer to our problems. Rachel would never be happy with the earl of Beresford."

But Veronica, to whom defeat had always been a stranger, turned a pair of sad eyes on her sister.

"For all Rachel's shyness she has always been a young lady of exceptional intelligence. It cannot be wrong for her to think ahead, preventing her children from suffering the exigencies of penury in which we were raised."

"But she doesn't love him!" Charlotte insisted. "Nor can you convince me she would be at all comfortable in the shallow, witty company with which the gentleman would fill his home."

Veronica's nerves were already irritated and she could not overlook Charlotte's disapproving emphasis on the word "witty."

"Oh, take your stuffy baron and be done with it," she snapped, turning and jerking her gown from the wardrobe.

"I have!"

"Charlotte!" Veronica whirled around, her eyes wide, her fit of temper forgotten. "He's declared himself?"

Charlotte nodded, her face glowing. "I must tell you I have been guilty of a deception."

"Oh?" Veronica said, half amused but still excited. "Go on, I pray."

"I had given the gentleman reason to believe you are most taken with him," Charlotte said, fumbling with the pair of gloves Veronica had chosen to wear and refusing to meet her sister's eyes. At another time Charlotte's hesitancy in admitting her deception would have brought out a high good humour in Veronica, and even now she could not resist a smile.

"My dear sister," she said, patting Charlotte's shoulder as she passed to lay the gown on a chair, "there is hope for your humanity yet."

Charlotte's colour rose; her discomfort brought on an excess of formality as she lowered her head, seemingly giving her attention to the carpet.

"I can quite see my part in the matter seems lacking in a certain delicacy—" determined to face the facts she raised her chin "—but indeed, he has been so attentive and so sensible of my need to forgo more strenuous pleasures like dancing."

Privately, Veronica thought the baron must look upon Charlotte's weak ankle as a convenient excuse to abjure frivolity, but she kept her opinion to herself.

"We have fallen into the habit of easy discourse, and last night at the ball I told him—and you will admit in that I was honest—that I had mistaken the direction of your sentiments."

"Excellent," Veronica said, as relieved to be free of the baron's advances as she was glad for her sister's happiness.

A soft smile was playing on Charlotte's narrow lips. "It seems he had already noted your interest in Beresford and had reached the same conclusion." She reached out and took Veronica's gown, stroking the satin in absent movement before she raised her head.

"He called this afternoon and asked if I would care for it if he spoke to Mama."

"Oh, dear Charlotte!" Veronica embraced her sister and felt her tremble. Veronica clung to her, glad at least one of them would be finding happiness.

"But not a word to anyone until he's spoken to Mama," Charlotte said. "Now you must dress."

They scurried about and Veronica was adding the last touches to her toilet when Lady Ellerbrook, followed by Rachel, also entered her chamber.

It took hardly a glance to warn both Veronica and Charlotte that something untoward was in the air. Not only was Lady Ellerbrook in a stammering flutter, but Rachel's blue-green eyes were wide with consternation and her face pale as death.

Practical even in times of severe stress, Veronica hurried past her mother to close the door and then stood with her back to it. It was Charlotte who demanded to know what was amiss.

"Amabelle has not returned...." As she spoke, Lady Ellerbrook's voice gained half an octave with every word. Her explanation ended in a wail and she sank onto a settle, giving way to the vapours.

Much affrighted and thinking some accident had befallen their sister, both Charlotte and Veronica turned to Rachel.

"She did not return with the Brentwoods from Richmond Park," Rachel said, and enlightened her sisters as to the events of the past half hour.

During tea Lady Ellerbrook had been nervous in the extreme. She had expected Amabelle home earlier, but she had assumed the party was dallying on the way back. When twilight deepened and there was still no word of Amabelle, Lady Ellerbrook had sent Martin to check with the Brentwoods.

They had assumed Amabelle had caught up with the Brentwood servants when she returned to the picnic area and had ridden back to Brook Street in the family carriage.

"Do you mean they did not ascertain whether she had arrived home safely?" Charlotte demanded.

Rachel twisted her hands helplessly and shook her head. "Martin could only report what she was told," she said, and removing a vinaigrette from her purse, attempted to offer her mother what solace she could.

"She is kidnapped or murdered," Lady Ellerbrook wailed, and raised her eyes to her two older daughters seeking their assurances that she had misread the matter.

Her mind already numbed with her own miseries, Veronica was bereft of any strength with which to comfort her mother, and Charlotte was in no better case. Then to add to their confusion, Martin tapped upon the door and entered swiftly. She had intercepted a footman coming above stairs with a message. The earl of Beresford and Lady Elizabeth were awaiting the family in the drawing room.

"You must tender our regrets," Charlotte said immediately.

Though much caught up in the emergency, Veronica was still aware of their social obligations. "No, we must go down. At least you and I," she said to Charlotte. "We are engaged to them this evening and we must make some suitable excuse."

They had entered the drawing room and were just exchanging pleasantries, not having yet had time to tender their regrets, when the door burst open and Amabelle, her bonnet askew, her face dirtied and streaked with tears, ran into the room and threw herself into Veronica's arms.

"Oh, it has been so dreadful! And I was so frightened!" she cried, burying her grimy face in Veronica's shoulder. "And though I meant to be good, I really did, I fear this time I have ruined us all!"

With great presence of mind, the earl strode to the doors and closed them firmly. Veronica led Amabelle to a *confidante* and seated her tearful sister. They were some minutes calming the youngest Miss Westfield until she could relate her harrowing story. Most fortunately what she saw as the magnitude of her indiscretion had been her chance encounter with the gentlemen on South Audley Street and therefore it was near the beginning of her tale.

With an abruptness Veronica could only consider unfeeling, the earl demanded that part of the story in more precise detail. When he was satisfied, he rose and strode from the room.

Amabelle related her story from beginning to end to her two sisters and Lady Elizabeth. And she was still in the midst of her apologies and her fears when Veronica instructed her to cease and requested Charlotte to remove her to her chamber.

Once Lady Elizabeth and Veronica were alone in the drawing room, Veronica was overcome and sat trembling. Though the basic sweetness of her nature was often hidden by the sharpness of her tongue, Lady Elizabeth showed herself most sensible of Veronica's concern. She suggested the situation was probably one that could be overcome with very little effort.

"You may not know them," Elizabeth said bracingly, "but I do believe I recognize the party she spoke of. We saw them at a distance as we turned onto Brook Street, though I expect they did not notice us. And the vicious-tongued park saunterer Amabelle described could have been none other than Mr. Clauson."

"Then we are indeed done for," Veronica said. "He delights in malicious stories, and not a fortnight ago Charlotte called him to task for it. He will have no hesitancy in destroying Amabelle's character."

"I doubt he would be much heeded."

"It would take very little to ruin Amabelle's chances for the future."

"Stuff!" Lady Elizabeth exclaimed. "She is a schoolroom chit and this little escapade will soon be forgotten."

"I hope most fervently you are right," Veronica said. "My mind is in such a muddle I cannot think. There is a limit to the number of problems I can face in a single day."

"Well, my reason for coming," Elizabeth said in a far more hesitant voice, "was to help clear your mind. What I must say is difficult." She looked up, her blue eyes dark with apprehension. "I want you to understand, we meant no harm."

"Harm?" Veronica could not imagine what admission her friend was about to make.

The pretty widow took a deep breath and rushed into the story of the wager. She spoke hurriedly, as if unsure she had the courage to finish.

"Understand, Julian never meant to capture her heart—nor is his engaged, so there is no possibility of an alliance between them...." Her voice was rising as she spoke. "Oh, but we did not mean to create such a tangle, please believe me."

Veronica sat, astounded as she heard Elizabeth's admission. Dimly she thought she should feel anger, but she was as yet unable to credit what she heard. Her only solace had been that Rachel would find happiness with the earl of Beresford. But if he held no affection for her, Rachel would suffer the same heartaches that now afflicted Veronica.

Correctly reading her look, Lady Elizabeth hastened to assure her that the earl had in no wise intended to engage the young lady's affection. He had set out simply to prove he could reduce her fear of him and cause her to enjoy his company.

But Veronica was remembering Rachel's unstinting praise of the gentleman.

"I am convinced after hearing her this very afternoon, that her heart has been won," Veronica said.

Lady Elizabeth stared at her with growing horror. "What have we done?" she murmured. "I must also tell you my brother, though as unwise in this affair as myself, is a man of honour. He would not thoughtlessly mislead her nor, if he realizes he has, will he walk away uncaring."

"You are saying," Veronica muttered, misery plain in her voice, "that if he has engaged Rachel's heart, he will offer for her?"

Lady Elizabeth nodded, quite as depressed as Veronica. "It would not be a successful alliance."

The ladies were sitting and sharing each other's unhappiness when the door to the drawing room opened again and Lord Beresford strode in and closed the door behind him. He strolled nonchalantly over and began pulling off his gloves, which he had neglected to leave in the entranceway.

"My dearest but most scatterbrained sister—" his voice held all the tones of languorous irritation "—I would advise you in the future to take greater care. When a young lady rides with you, it is really most thoughtless of you to lose her on the way home."

"What?" Shocked out of her earlier doldrums, Lady Elizabeth stared up at her brother.

"Yes, indeed," he said. "You might be interested in the latest *on dit*. You invited young Miss Amabelle Westfield to ride with you this afternoon. Then you became separated for no more reason than the resulting confusion when two public hacks collided. In your attempts to avoid an embarrassing contretemps, you lost the young lady before you could escort her home."

"Julian, what are you saying?"

"Quite fortunately, you set me to searching for her. By the way she is still not overly familiar with the local area." He paused and, reaching in his pocket for his snuffbox, took a pinch. "I, for my part, was fortunate enough to encounter six gentlemen on their way to Cribbs Parlour. They were able to assure me that the young lady had indeed found her way and when last seen was approaching the protection of her home with as much haste as was seemly."

"Julian!" Elizabeth jumped to her feet and, standing on tiptoe, planted a kiss on her brother's cheek. "You have been positively brilliant!"

"I thought so," he said, disengaging his sleeve from her clutch and replacing his snuffbox. "And that, my dear, will only cost you an evening at the theatre. Since I believe Miss Westfield was on the point of expressing her regrets...?" He raised an eyebrow in query to Veronica, who nodded.

"Then we would have found the entertainment sadly flat. It's just as well that you are so upset over having lost the youngest Miss Westfield that you are at this moment at home, prostrate with hysterics."

"Hysterics!" Elizabeth said, in some agitation. "I have never succumbed—"

"My dear, you have hysterics," her brother corrected her.

"Oh, very well."

Veronica, who had listened to this exchange with doubt, dawning hope and then the certainty that Amabelle's mischance would not lead to scandal, could not contain her own gratitude. Following Elizabeth's example much more literally than she had intended, she stepped forward and kissed the earl on the other cheek. Then, realizing the impropriety of her action, she blushed and dissolved into the most exquisite confusion.

As Veronica flushed, Lady Elizabeth attempted to cover her friend's embarrassment by asking a practical question concerning the earl's tale.

"Though I can see how we could have become separated during a contretemps between two jarveys, it passes my understanding how we could have widened the distance between us sufficiently to allow Amabelle to become lost."

"Oh, there's no problem with that," the earl said tranquilly, after a long gaze at Veronica. "You, my dear, were so henwitted as to allow your mount to run away with you."

"Absolutely not!" Elizabeth insisted. "That part of the story you must change."

"Unfortunately, Bess, it must be your horse that ran away with you," Beresford repeated. "If there *is* talk about the Misses Westfield—" and he gave a congratulatory bow to Veronica as he spoke "—the conversation is entirely devoted to their excellent horsemanship and their spirited animals."

"I do hope," Lady Elizabeth said in accents of martyrdom, though laughter twinkled in her eyes, "I do hope, dear Veronica, that you will keep that young lady under control in the future. My reputation can stand only so much.''

Veronica's gratitude to Lady Elizabeth and Lord Beresford was in no way diminished, but her embarrassment over having so effusively shown her thankfulness caused her to look forward to their leavetaking. She did not bid them stay when, some moments later, they rose to leave.

''I daresay I shall spend the evening with some elevating reading,'' Lady Elizabeth said in die-away accents, though a smile indicated she had no such fatal intention, even if she did resort to a book.

The remark brought the baron to the forefront of Veronica's thoughts, and with it a question.

''Surely we are not the only members of your theatre party?''

''The gentlemen...'' the earl murmured, struck with an unwelcome memory. ''It seems that I suffer, too, as I shall be obliged to provide other entertainment for them.'' Suddenly his lips twitched.

''Julian, what are you planning?'' Lady Elizabeth demanded.

''Something wholly unfit for your ears, dear Bess. I'm sorely tempted to provide an evening that will either increase or cure Mr. Tonley's stammer and send the baron home with a genuine need for inspirational reading—no, you definitely should not inquire.''

Veronica's spirits were raised by the lighter atmosphere accompanying the departure of the earl and his sister, but once the door closed behind them, she was anxious to learn what was taking place above stairs. She was in dread of finding that either Amabelle or her mother had given way to hysteria. But though she paused at the doors of both rooms on her way to her own, all was quiet.

Charlotte was watching for Veronica, and opened her door, motioning her inside.

"I persuaded Mama to take a sedative and also had one prepared for Amabelle," she said. "We can pass a quiet night, but what we face on the morrow I dare not think."

"If the earl has read the situation aright, I am convinced we have little to concern us," Veronica said and favoured Charlotte with an account of the earl and Lady Elizabeth's attempts to prevent a scandal.

Her mouth still prim with disapproval and anxiety, Charlotte was nevertheless sensible of Lord Beresford's efforts. She was generous in praise of his quick thinking, which had saved them a forced departure from London.

"His ingenuity will succeed only if the Brentwoods do not speak up," Charlotte said. "I'd not trust them to keep quiet when Amabelle cuts the acquaintance."

"They will," Veronica countered Charlotte's pessimism. "They could not endanger her reputation without admitting to leaving her in the most odious circumstances. Even if the officers in their party were to talk, they would find themselves cut from the invitation lists of society."

"That's true," Charlotte said with a relieved sigh.

"It's Lord Beresford who deserves our gratitude for saving Amabelle's reputation and our name," Veronica said, determined to impress upon Charlotte their indebtedness to the earl.

"I will inform you straight out that I cannot approve of his fascination with levity or these most unseemly—rigs—" She pronounced the word as if it had left a bad taste in her mouth. "But only an ingrate would deny he has been most obliging in our difficulty. He handled the situation in the best manner possible."

"Just so. I will take myself to bed now," Veronica said, hurrying out of Charlotte's room. If she had to endure many more of her sister's animadversions upon the earl's character, Veronica was not sure she could maintain her composure. Even when she was giving him credit for having saved their reputations, Charlotte could not keep from criticizing him. It was enough to send Veronica into a strong fit of irritation.

She would be glad when Charlotte married her pompous baron. And moreover, while she might love her sister dearly, she fervently hoped Charlotte's future visits to Red Oaks would be infrequent and short.

CHAPTER ELEVEN

THE NEXT MORNING Veronica woke early and rang for her breakfast tray. She was drinking her second cup of chocolate when the bedroom door opened and Lady Ellerbrook entered. The good lady's hair was covered by a lace cap and she wore a wrapper over her night-dress as she came softly over to Veronica's bedside.

"I have passed a night of most exquisite horror," she murmured, "not awake enough to think yet . . ."

Veronica leaned forward and patted her mother's plump little hand, feeling the tremor, slight enough not to be discerned by the eye, but most definitely there at the touch. "I was remiss in not bringing the news last night but I didn't want to disturb you," she said. "We have been most fortunate. The quick thinking of Lord Beresford has saved Amabelle and us from possible scandal."

Lady Ellerbrook sat wide-eyed as Veronica began the full tale of Amabelle's adventures, but she was in-terrupted before she had scarcely begun. Both awak-ening early, Rachel and Charlotte joined them, their trays of chocolate and rolls following in the hands of their maids. Within a few minutes, four of the five Westfield ladies were sitting on Veronica's bed shar-ing an early-morning repast. Veronica and Charlotte told Rachel and their mother of Amabelle's harrowing experiences, and repeated the tale of Lord Beresford's efforts on the child's behalf.

"We should wake her and tell her," Rachel said. "Even though she slept the night in a sedated state, her rest cannot have been more than indifferent."

"No, let her sleep," Charlotte adjured Rachel. "I doubt any of us plan on leaving the house this morning and she can be told as soon as she awakens. I can see it would be too cruel to do so, but I have considered leaving her to suffer the pangs of fright for a day or so. But I daresay we must tell her that the situation is not so desperate as she first supposed."

"We surely must," Veronica announced with a sharp look at Charlotte. "She has learned her lesson most forcibly. Her fault was thoughtlessness. She has never had a deliberate disregard for proprieties."

But while they were speaking, Martin entered the room and approached the bed. In her expression they read a proclamation of doom. With a shaking hand she held out a folded paper. Upon one side Veronica's name, blurred in the middle by moisture but still readable, was written in the large round characters of a schoolgirl.

"She has gone," Martin stated, giving verbal evidence of what the note portended.

The four ladies stared at the maid in shocked silence. Then, feeling she had been used by the volatile Amabelle past the point of reason, Veronica slapped the coverlet with her hand and announced that Amabelle might go to the devil for all she cared.

This remark, coming close on the heels of the knowledge that her youngest daughter had involved herself in yet another escapade, threw Lady Ellerbrook into the vapours and Martin intervened.

"If you will forgive me for saying so, this time the situation may not be so desperate. She has taken Carey with her."

"Carey?" Veronica repeated blankly.

"One of the new housemaids," Charlotte said. "As silly a little goose as one could find, letting Amabelle fill her head with a lot of nonsense."

"And I'd say that's what happened," Martin replied. "It was because I could not find Carey and entered Miss Amabelle's room that I found the note."

She gazed pointedly at the paper in Veronica's hands and announced her intention of retiring to Rachel's chambers should she be needed later. With the tact of an old and valued servant, she withdrew to leave the family in the privacy such occasions demanded.

Martin had hardly closed the door when Charlotte, in a show of energy not apparent in her since she was nine years old, bounced a little on the bed. "Read it, Veronica," she admonished. "I have not the slightest doubt she has eloped with some officer in a foot regiment."

This opinion brought another wail from Lady Ellerbrook. Her lamentations ceased as Veronica opened the note and read aloud in a choked voice.

My Dearest Sister,
I cannot by words Convince you of my Deepest Regret at having been involved in a Scandal that

must Reflect upon our Name. Though I am certain you will Not believe it, the Circumstances were not of my Making.

But since I cannot undo the Damage in any other manner, I am returning to Red Oaks and you must put it about that in your Disapproval of my Actions, I have been Banished from London, never to be Allowed in Polite Circles again.

Believe me, Dearest Sister, it was never my intention to cause you the slightest Distress.

Your Wayward, but Loving and Most Regretful sister,

Amabelle

Before she had finished reading, Veronica's anger had entirely drained away. As she had prophesied to Charlotte the night before, Amabelle had learned from her experience. It had not occurred to them that the child would be so distraught as to remove herself completely from society.

Lady Ellerbrook dissolved into tears again. Rachel, too, began to cry, and even Charlotte was dabbing at her eyes.

Veronica viewed the response of her family imperfectly as a mist clouded her own vision, but her nature demanded action. She energetically forced her bed tray into the weeping Charlotte's hands and struggled from beneath her bed covers.

"Rachel," she ordered, "go straight to your room and bring Martin here. Charlotte, come and help me," she demanded.

But encumbered by not only her own, but also Veronica's tray, her sister required assistance to remove herself from the bed. "What are you planning to do?" Charlotte asked as Veronica took one of the trays and set it on the small chair.

"We have awakened early," said Veronica, throwing a hurried glance at the clock on the mantlepiece. "And it is possible we can yet stop her. She could not have left the house in time to catch the night mail, and there may still be a chance we can prevent her from boarding a stage."

At that moment Martin entered the room behind Charlotte, only to leave almost immediately, having been adjured by Veronica to discover from below stairs the location and departure time of the nearest stage.

"Bring your cloak with you and have the porter procure a hack," Veronica added as Martin was leaving.

That morning there was no time for dressers. Clothing was scattered all over the room as Rachel, Charlotte and Lady Ellerbrook attempted to assist Veronica. She could have dressed faster alone, but the others were pathetically anxious to help her on her way to intercept Amabelle. Despite the fact that her mother, in her distress, kept trying to push a pair of formal gloves on her eldest daughter, Veronica was finally ready.

She was just fastening her pelisse while Charlotte held out a bonnet, when Martin re-entered the room. She came with the information that the High Flier was due to leave the Saracen's Head at nine o'clock. Located on Aldgate High Street, the inn was not many

minutes away; but even if the hack were already waiting at the door, the stage could have left the inn well
before Veronica arrived.

Unfortunately, early morning was an unfashionable time for society to be about, so there was a scarc-
ity of hacks in Mayfair. The footmen scurried in several directions in an attempt to locate a vehicle. One
thoughtfully ran to the stables and called for a carriage to be put to. Veronica paced on the walk in front
of the house, ignoring Martin's pleas that she step
back inside to await the arrival of a conveyance.

She espied a horseman coming down the street
heading in the direction of Hyde Park, and easily recognized Lord Beresford.

He was a gentleman with a quick eye and immediately noted certain signs indicating hasty dress.
Veronica's impatient pacing and the oddity of her
being upon the street at such an unusual hour was
enough to enable him to take in the situation and its
probable cause without delay.

"What's that silly chit done now?" he demanded as
he brought his horse to a halt.

Veronica might have resented that question from
any other, but she appreciated the earl's ready understanding. She found in it some solace for her agitation.

"Indeed, sir, the fault was ours," she said.
"Thinking her deeply asleep, we did not inform her
that you had been so helpful." She then went on to tell
him what had occurred.

"You'll not make Aldgate High Street in time to
catch the Flier now," he said, pulling out a large gold

watch and considering the time. "Step back into the house and await me there. We'll need a chaise to catch her at Blalock, where they change horses. I'll return for you with my phaeton."

Seeing the sense of what the earl suggested, Veronica strove to thank him, but before she could do so, he wheeled his mount and galloped back up the street. Her impatience caused time to drag, but in less than a quarter of an hour she heard the clatter of horses and vehicles coming down the street. From the window she glimpsed the earl of Beresford. He drove his racing phaeton and was followed by a chaise and four.

She and Martin hurried out only to find the earl in some argument with his diminutive tiger. The servant was threatening to give notice if he was forced to abandon his post in the phaeton and ride in the chaise with a lady's maid.

Veronica expostulated with the earl, saying that she would be just as comfortable in the chaise, and Martin added her mite considering it unseemly that her young lady should be seen in a racing vehicle.

The earl was inflexible. "If we outdistance the chaise," he explained once he had helped Veronica into the phaeton and they were bowling along the deserted streets of Mayfair, "your presence will be needed to get Amabelle off the stage. She will not come for me alone."

"I confess I had not thought of that," Veronica replied. "Having met you but once, she could not be thought backward in hesitating to accept your company."

"Just so. And if her maid should set up a screech, I would be hard put for an explanation," the earl said, a gleam in his eye.

Seeing his amusement, Veronica attempted to give at least the appearance of matching it. She was hard pressed; her concern over Amabelle and her discomfort at being in the earl's company had thrown her mind into a whirl. She did not think herself capable of handling her side in a witty conversation. Nevertheless, she felt she must try. Although the earl had not been in the least hesitant in assisting her in the present difficulty, he could not but be bored with the Westfields and their problems. It behooved her to help lighten the burden.

"I see just how it is," she said. "My family back on Brook Street is doubtless singing your praises, but I am persuaded I should withhold my gratitude until I discover what price I am to pay."

They had by now left the busier market section behind, and Lord Beresford dropped the ribbons, giving the team their heads. The quick glance he threw at Veronica held both surprise and humour.

"Do you imagine, dear girl, I am for hire?"

Busy bracing herself for the increased speed, Veronica nodded emphatically.

"I most assuredly do, my lord, but you would never take such mundane recompense as coin of the realm. Let me see if I can discover what your newest rig might be. If I am not to suffer the company of Lord Folkestone on the return journey—" Veronica's ruminating was interrupted by a crack of laughter from the earl "—then possibly I am to ride back in an ox cart, chaperoned by a crate of chickens for your edification—''

"No, not chickens," the earl objected, "they would be penned and easily ignored. Sheep. Or pigs, maybe—"

"Pigs, by all means," Veronica agreed. "You must know I am exceedingly fond of sheep, and before the cart had progressed half a mile, I would have made a number of new friends."

Veronica expected the earl to continue the joke and was somewhat surprised when no other remark was forthcoming. And they rode for some two miles in silence before he lifted his gaze from the road and turned to search her face.

"Is something amiss, my lord?" she asked, not sure what this change of his mood portended.

"Not amiss," the earl said slowly. "I am filled with admiration."

"Sir?" Veronica was not sure she had heard him correctly.

"You are remarkably calm." He paused, adjusting his pressure on the reins as they approached a curve in the road. "I'd half expected a case of the vapours."

"I cannot think tears would speed us along the way," Veronica murmured, wishing he had not mentioned a possible break in her composure. She was desperately striving against that very thing.

"It is refreshing to be acquainted with a young lady of both sense and control when she finds herself in a difficult position."

Though Veronica told herself the joking had been to keep the earl from ennui, once the conversation turned serious, she realized the humorous remarks had been the thin stitching holding her own composure together. After his compliment, she blinked away the moisture gathering in her eyes. She turned her head to hide her rising emotions, but she could not prevent the catch in her voice.

"Then I beg you, my lord, continue with your levity, for I very much fear you credit me with too much strength of character. Should I let my mind dwell upon that child in the coach, I may give you a disgust of me."

"You would not be goosish to give way to tears," Beresford said. "I can tell you exactly how it is. At the moment she is suffering the exquisite joys of misery, seeing her self-sacrificing effort as one that will not remain secret but will at some future time become known to society." The earl's remark so perfectly matched Amabelle's thinking that Veronica stared at him in dismay, wondering if he could have overheard one of Amabelle's tantrums.

"And society will be wrung to the withers," Beresford continued. "They will learn of her heroic efforts to protect the good name of her sisters. And when she returns for her season, the ton will welcome her as a true heroine, meeting her with open arms and open hearts—"

"Oh, you must stop!" Veronica said, unable to control a trill of laughter. "Sir, I hold strongly to my regard for your good character. If I did not I would believe you have been behind the curtains in the drawing room. Unless—" and her eyes widened with consternation "—it cannot be that Amabelle has been so unthinking as to show the intensity of her spirit in public—'' She gripped the seat in horror.

The earl gave another crack of laughter. "I doubt it, since no such gossip has come to my ears. Remember, Bess was once her age. It's my own sister I portray. From the grousing of friends I have no doubt the age of sixteen wears a uniform of the mistreated heroine as strict as that of the Life Guard.

"And I'll tell you something else," the earl continued. "For the next week at least, dear Amabelle will have difficulty in forgiving you for making her grand gesture unnecessary."

"She will," Veronica agreed, caught up by the mood of the earl's portrayal. "But I welcome your admission about your sister. It almost gives me hope. I cannot speak for myself on being sixteen, for one does not see oneself truly, but neither Charlotte nor Rachel ever behaved so, and I was beginning to despair of Amabelle."

"But they, my dear, were not sixteen in London, within a year of their come-outs and chafing at the delay."

"True." Veronica nodded. "If Amabelle will grow out of her uncontrollable spirits and become anything like Lady Elizabeth, I much look forward to her maturity. I confess I find your sister delightful."

At that remark the earl gave her a look of humorous affection. "A sentiment I share," Beresford said.

"I will have need of some delight in my family," Veronica went on, "for Charlotte daily becomes more like Folkestone. I tell you in confidence that they have reached an understanding. I love my sister, but when she becomes Lady Folkestone, I heartily desire they will move to Australia.''

The earl chuckled. ''Between the prosing Folkestone and the stammering Tonley I have no doubt *you* will be transported to Australia. You will certainly murder one or the other.''

Veronica gave him a quick look. Certainly Mr. Tonley had been entirely removed from the scene since Beresford had entered Rachel's life.

''Oh, I hardly think that gentleman is of any concern,'' Veronica said and bit her tongue. Did she dare give him a hint of Rachel's feelings? With her own heart so engaged, she quailed at the thought, but the earl was already shaking his head in adamant denial.

''Mark my words, she'll have Tonley,'' he said. ''Rachel is as sweet as you would have me believe, but I find her conversation, which centres entirely on that young man, boring in the extreme.''

Veronica stared at him. ''She talks to you about Tonley?''

''How not? What else would loosen that shy tongue of hers?'' A sudden understanding seemed to light his eyes and his smile widened. ''You cannot have thought my interest lay in Rachel nor hers in me?''

''But—'' There was nothing for it. Veronica had to tell him the truth, unpalatable to her as it might be.

''I must tell you, my lord,'' she said slowly, ''that Rachel's conversation at home is turned entirely upon you.''

Favouring her with another smile, the earl nodded emphatically. ''And how not?'' he said again. ''Your sister may be shy, but she does not lack spirit.''

As they were at that time approaching the small village of Barnet, the earl was forced to turn his attention to slowing the team. His explanation then came in snips only as his mind could be spared.

"And if you believe she took it kindly when she learned you must lend a hand in making her a match, you're far off your mark."

"You mean you told her what was toward?" Veronica demanded, aghast.

Lord Beresford drew the team to the side of the road to avoid a roaming cow dragging its tether rope and stake behind it. When he whipped up the horses again, he gave her a teasing glance.

"Of course! You cannot have thought me such a loose screw that I would lead her on? While Bess was pulling a rig on me, Charlotte was attempting to manage your life, and you Rachel's, is it too much for her to take a part once she knew the plot?"

"She's been humbugging me?" Veronica gasped. The enormity of the situation caused her eyes to stare and her mouth to fall open.

"By the look on your face, I'd say she has been successful. She was perfectly willing when she discovered you were trying to separate her from her stammerer."

Relief rushed over Veronica like a wave. For some moments she could say nothing, so great was her joy that her unwise original plans were at last brought to an end.

They had whirled through Barnet in a cloud of dust and Beresford was again urging on the horses when he spoke.

"And I wonder if you are right in your disapproval of Tonley," Beresford went on. "Behind that stammer is a good understanding. He's a bit provincial for my taste, but he will provide his wife with all the luxuries. Like Rachel, he's not enamoured of society and will give her the quiet life she wants. It's not common knowledge, but as well as being his father's only heir, he's in line for some valuable properties in his mother's family. His children will come into the world hosed and shod."

"I had no idea," Veronica answered automatically. Not being one to value a person by his wealth, she was giving less thought to the information than to the fact that the earl was so knowledgeable.

"I wonder how you came to be so informed about Mr. Tonley's circumstances, if they're not well-known."

The earl cast her a wary look; he suddenly found it necessary to sort out the ribbons, giving particular attention to the exact tension of each of the eight strips of leather. His silent absorption warned Veronica that there was more behind his pronouncements concerning Mr. Tonley than she had originally supposed.

"Sir, must I rephrase my remark into a direct question?"

The earl cleared his throat; his poise seemed to be in tatters. "I—er—I think he was trying out his speech before he approached Lady Ellerbrook."

"Before he—" Veronica found herself hardly able to speak. "You cannot mean that after seeing your attentions to Rachel he would think there was the slightest use in his pressing his suit?"

Veronica turned an indignant look on the earl and felt her face go hot at his delighted laughing glance. To cover her confusion she turned away, not wanting him to see how her own words had affected her.

"My girl, you are singularly goosish on one subject, and I pray you will never come to your senses," he said softly. "You so set up my self-esteem that I have room for only one thought. How could Tonley or Folkestone be such flats as even to notice other females when you were present?"

Veronica clutched the armrest and the edge of the seat as if her pounding heart would bounce her out of the fast-moving phaeton.

"Me?" she murmured breathlessly. "I will admit, sir, that few females are so tall and gangly and lacking in—"

"Lacking in guile, in pretence, but so full of laughter and wit." Beresford finished for her. "Shallow beauty fades, but a fine mind can make for a life of unending delight." He paused again, his voice turning hesitant. "I wasn't perfectly candid with you about Tonley. He is more perceptive than I thought, and he never considered me a rival. He came to me with his petition for Rachel's hand, sure I was already accepted as the head of the Westfield family."

"He came to you—" Veronica was strongly reminded of a parrot with her constant repetitions.

Beresford was giving his attention to the ribbons again. When he spoke his voice was hoarse with tension.

"Shall we make it true? Is that school still so important?"

"What school?" Veronica asked, for a moment not understanding what he meant, and then she remembered. Her laugh was sudden, startling the horses. By the side of the road a leaf, disturbed by the speeding vehicle, fluttered and drifted, moving away as lightly as her dreams for Red Oaks Seminary—which had been fading, had she stopped to examine her desires, since she first met the earl.

"What school..." she said again, but the words were not a question. They were the answer to the earl's proposal, and his smile showed he took it as such. He raised his hands as if to draw up the phaeton and then thought better of it.

"Plague take those sisters of ours!" he snapped. "Here I've proposed and I can't even stop this vehicle to kiss you."

"Sir, you are becoming the head of the family after all." Veronica smiled. "At least you have no trouble with your sister."

"You think not? Once we get your affairs settled, I think I'll marry that chit off, though how, I don't see. She is too fond of her freedom to trade her heart. She'll lead us a merry chase before she settles down, but one sister at a time— Oh, we've caught the runaway."

They had rounded a turn in the road and came suddenly upon the High Flier, which had slowed as the driver turned the coach into the inn yard to change horses. But though they had caught up with Amabelle earlier than expected, Veronica had no thought for her sister, who stared in wonder as she saw the phaeton flash by and draw to a halt on the other side of the yard.

The earl paid no attention to the stage. As a stable boy rushed forward, Beresford tossed him the reins and whirled to face Veronica, who was surprised by his sudden movement. His eyes had lost their laughter.

"Will you close your mouth?" he said. "I have no desire to kiss your teeth."

Veronica immediately obeyed and the stage yard was treated to the sight of a tonnish pair in a public embrace. Unmindful of the audible remarks, the earl held Veronica in his arms. The disembarking passengers gave it as their opinion that such behaviour was totally beyond the bounds of propriety.

Veronica slowly and reluctantly disengaged herself and glanced around at the staring faces, too overcome with happiness to be discomposed by their curiosity, amusement or disapproval. Then suddenly the ridiculousness of the situation struck her and she reached up to straighten her bonnet.

"My lord," she admonished him, "we have been remiss in not thinking up a proper excuse for removing Amabelle from the stage." Her voice shook with suppressed laughter. "It would not do to cause a scene and start talk."

Adjusting his neck cloth, the earl nodded, at his most urbane. "Public notice is a thing I most abhor," he remarked, while the corner of his mouth fought a recalcitrant smile. "But should we put our heads together, I think we must contrive."

Veronica was sure they would.

PAMELA BROWNING

...is fireworks on the green at the Fourth of July and prayers said around the Thanksgiving table. It is the dream of freedom realized in thousands of small towns across this great nation.

But mostly, the Heartland is its people. People who care about and help one another. People who cherish traditional values and give to their children the greatest gift, the gift of love.

American Romance presents HEARTLAND, an emotional trilogy about people whose memories, hopes and dreams are bound up in the acres they farm.

HEARTLAND... the story of America.

Don't miss these heartfelt stories: American Romance #237 SIMPLE GIFTS (March), #241 FLY AWAY (April), and #245 HARVEST HOME (May).

HRT-1

HARLEQUIN SIGNATURE EDITION

Penny Jordan

Stronger than Yearning

He was the man of her dreams!

The same dark hair, the same mocking eyes; it was as if the Regency rake of the portrait, the seducer of Jenna's dream, had come to life. Jenna, believing the last of the Deverils dead, was determined to buy the great old Yorkshire Hall—to claim it for her daughter, Lucy, and put to rest some of the painful memories of Lucy's birth. She had no way of knowing that a direct descendant of the black sheep Deveril even existed—or that James Allingham and his own powerful yearnings would disrupt her plan entirely.

Penny Jordan's first Harlequin Signature Edition *Love's Choices* was an outstanding success. Penny Jordan has written more than 40 best-selling titles—more than 4 million copies sold.

Now, be sure to buy her latest bestseller, *Stronger Than Yearning*. Available wherever paperbacks are sold—in June.

Harlequin American Romance

Romances that go one step farther...
American Romance

Realistic stories involving people you can relate to and care about.

Compelling relationships between the mature men and women of today's world.

Romances that capture the core of genuine emotions between a man and a woman.

Join us each month for four new titles wherever paperback books are sold.
Enter the world of American Romance.